THE
TEDDY BEAR HABIT

THE
TEDDY BEAR HABIT

James Lincoln Collier

HYPERION

NEW YORK

For Geoffrey

Text copyright © 1967 by James L. Collier

First published by Grosset & Dunlap, Inc. © 1967. Reprinted by permission of the author.

Volo and the Volo colophon are trademarks of Disney Enterprises, Inc. All rights reserved. No part of this book may be reproduced or transmitted in any form or by any means, electronic or mechanical, including photocopying, recording, or by any information storage and retrieval system, without written permission from the publisher. For information address Volo Books, 114 Fifth Avenue, New York, New York 10011-5690.

First Volo edition © 2001
1 3 5 7 9 10 8 6 4 2

Printed in the United States of America
The text for this book is set in 13-point Deepdene

ISBN 0-7868-1543-4 (special promotion)
ISBN 0-7868-1544-2 (pbk.)
Library of Congress Catalog Card Number: 00-46171

Visit www.volobooks.com

CHAPTER ONE

N SATURDAY morning we waited in line out in an alley behind the theater, about two hundred kids, some older than I, some younger, but mostly twelve or thirteen, about my age. The line went along the side of the building to a little flight of cement steps that led up to the stage door. At the top of the steps stood an old man with a face the color of a speckled banana. Every few minutes he would shout, "Next, come along, boy." The kid at the head of the line would jump as if he'd gotten jabbed. He'd run up the steps and disappear through the stage door.

The kids at the rear end of the line, where I was, were slugging each other and horsing around and so forth, but at the end near the stage door they were nervous and quiet. All of us were wearing clean white shirts and snap-on neckties and pants with creases and shoes with shines. Most had their mothers with them, or their fathers, or maybe their aunts or something. I had my voice teacher, Mr. Smythe-Jones. My mother died a long time ago, when I was just a baby, and my father was on deadline for *Smash Comics* and had to stay home and draw a sequence of Amorpho Man. He wouldn't have come anyway. He isn't that kind of a guy. I didn't care. Besides, Mr. Smythe-Jones always takes his voice students to these auditions.

They were choosing kids for parts in a Broadway show. They were making a musical comedy out of *Winnie the Pooh* and they needed a lot of kids. It wasn't likely that I'd get the part of Pooh or even Piglet. They would have some big stars for those parts. Besides, I wasn't that good. I'd only been studying voice with Mr. Smythe-Jones for a year or so. Still, I figured I might have a chance for Baby Roo or at least one of Rabbit's Friends and Relations.

I admit that *Winnie the Pooh* sounds very square, but being in a Broadway show is cool. You get famous around your school, and you can slouch around the cafeteria with your hands in your pockets saying things like, "Ringo told this friend of mine . . ." or "This time Murray the K came backstage, and . . ." Besides, you make a pile of loot, which is great even though your father steals it from you and puts it in a savings account in a bank someplace in Alaska or Hawaii, where you can't get it. So you can understand why this whole mass of kids were there all shaped up in their best clothes.

Mr. Smythe-Jones chewed mint-flavored Life Savers all the time. It drove me right out of my skull. When he leaned over you the way he did, you'd get a whiff that would bring the tears to your eyes. Mr. Smythe-Jones talked like an English duke on television. He talked with his mouth closed, as if he was afraid his teeth would fall out if he opened up too wide. He had a pink skull and a fancy mustache, and he always carried an umbrella, even on beautiful days. He liked to wave it around like a sword.

"What have you got in the bag, old chap?" I was carrying a paper bag.

"My gym clothes," I lied. I began to blush. "I'm going down to the Y and shoot baskets after."

"Here, I'll hold it for you, old boy," he said, flipping a candy wrapper off the sidewalk with the point of his umbrella.

I didn't look at him. "That's all right, I'll hold it," I said.

"You cahn't audition holding a bag, don't chew know."

"That's all right," I said. I felt very hot and was beginning to sweat. "I'll put it down somewhere just before I go on."

He started to argue with me some more, and then he stopped. He didn't want to make me nervous so I'd foul up. Whenever one of Mr.

Smythe-Jones's students gets into a show or on television or something he puts himself down as manager and cheats the kid out of half of his money.

But it didn't matter, because I was bound to get nervous anyway. It was just a question of how nervous I'd get. The line was moving along pretty quickly. I was getting down toward the little flight of cement stairs which led up to the stage door. Soon I'd walk up them, and out into the middle of a huge stage where I'd have to stand all alone and sing a song called "Without a Song," which is a pretty stupid thing to be singing when you're singing. Mr. Smythe-Jones had taken me to two other auditions. I knew what it would be like. Out front, lounging around on the theater seats, would be the author of the show and the man who wrote the music and the director and the producer and a half dozen other important people who would decide my fate. I'd walk out there and start singing, and about thirty seconds later my voice would crack, or I'd forget the words, or I'd just generally faint all over the place.

That's the way I am. That's my problem. I'm a loser. Anyone is likely to get a little bit nervous in a situation like that, but with me it isn't a little bit. I just fall apart. I get started off all right, usually. Then gradually I start getting nervous, and right away I begin to goof up. At first a little goof, and then a bigger one and so forth so that by the time I get down to the end the whole thing is completely ruined.

I've been that way ever since I can remember. I remember once when I was a little kid we had a spelling bee. I was zipping along, shooting the answers hardly without thinking. Then all of a sudden it dawned on me that there was only one other kid left, and that I had a good chance of winning. The minute I realized that I went hot and prickly and began to sweat. Naturally on the next turn I messed up "pinecone," which I knew exactly how to spell.

Or just last month. I go up to the Y and shoot baskets a lot, and this time some of the bigger guys were scrimmaging and they were short one man and they let me in. As long as I sort of hung back and fed the ball to the guys on my team I was fine. Then we got a fast break going, and all of a sudden I was dribbling into the basket alone. The minute I realized what was happening I got very embarrassed, and when I went up to shoot, I flung the ball over the back board. Nobody said anything, but man was I disgusted with myself, and pretty soon I quit and went down and had a shower. To miss a shot like that isn't a big thing. It's just an example of the way I am.

Once, when I was a real little kid—five, or something—Pop gave me a dime and told me to go into the candy store and get whatever I wanted. I went there; but I just couldn't get myself into the store. All I had to do was walk in, lay down the dime, and choose a candy bar, but I couldn't do it. I was so ashamed of myself that I ran up to the park and hid between a bush and a trash basket for two hours until Pop had the cops out looking for me. I can still remember that smell of an old half-eaten peach that was in the basket; all I have to do is see an advertisement for peach ice cream and I practically get the heaves.

You see: I'm a loser. Nobody knows I'm a loser. You can't tell it just by looking at me. But I know it.

I had gotten down near the flight of cement stairs at the beginning of the line. Back behind us the kids were shouting and horsing around, but here we were quiet. All around the bottom of the steps it was knee-deep in chewing-gum wrappers. Everybody was chewing like crazy. The kid just in front of me had on a pair of cool green suede shoes, and his face was a color to match. The kid at the head of the line was sort of leaning against the iron-pipe stair railing just as casual and cool as if he were home watching television, but his smile looked as if it was sewed on his face. I was specializing in sweat and hot flashes.

Mr. Smythe-Jones put his hand on my paper bag. "Here, old boy, I'll take it now," he said.

I didn't let go. "I got it, Mr. Smythe-Jones."

Suddenly the door at the top of the stairs slammed open. The man stuck out his banana-colored face and hollered, "Next boy, come along." The kid with the sewed-on smile shot up the stairs and disappeared through the door. The rest of us moved up one. "What did you say was in the bag, old chap?"

"I said before, my sneakers and stuff," I said.

"Don't chew know, you cahn't go on stage with sneaks, old fellow."

"I'll just stick it somewhere." A big cold ball of sweat rolled down my side like a snowball. My stomach was beginning slowly to clench and unclench. About a century before, when I had been back near the happy end of the line and hadn't any serious troubles, I had eaten a choco-late coconut bar. Now all the coconut had swollen up like a balloon and was trying to get out my throat. I kept wondering what was going to happen when I opened my mouth to sing.

Mr. Smythe-Jones laid his hand on the paper bag again. "Sure you wouldn't rather I held it, old bean?"

"It's just my sneakers," I said. "I don't want to lose them. I'll just put them down somewhere when I get inside."

Then the door slammed open once more. The boy with the green shoes and face straightened up as if he'd been shot full of electricity, ran up the steps, and disappeared through the door. Now I was next.

I stood at the bottom of the little flight of steps wishing that instead of a stage door at the top, there was a gallows. Hanging would have been less painful and a whole lot quicker. I wished I was one of those fellows who had stolen the Hermes Sapphire from the museum. They were bound to get caught and go to jail, where they wouldn't ever have to do any auditions. Of course there was the chance that the theater would catch fire in the next two minutes. Or maybe an atomic bomb would go off in Times Square, two blocks away, and I would be instantly demolished.

I was clutching at straws and I knew it; so I clutched my paper bag tighter and waited.

Of course there were no sneakers in it. There was no towel and no gym shorts, either. What I had in the bag was a worn-out, beat-up, patched old teddy bear with one of its glass eyes missing and the threads that made up its mouth mostly rubbed away. It was a little smaller than a football, and I had owned it all my life. Really, all of my life. Pop bought it for me the day I was born. Of course I didn't actually get it until I came home from the hospital, but I actually owned it from the first day of my life. It was as old as I was, older, even, because it must have been made sometime before I was born.

The truth is that I don't own it. It owns me. The thing is, I discovered a long time ago that I wasn't so much of a loser when I had the teddy bear around. It's magical. For example, that time I goofed up in the spelling bee. If I'd had the teddy there where I could have gotten a look at him, I wouldn't have goofed. I would have gotten nervous maybe, but I probably would have gotten the answer right. I don't understand it. I just feel stronger and more confident when he's around. I can't explain it. He's nothing but some cloth and a lot of old cotton batting. There shouldn't be any magic in that. But there is. Of course, a lot of the time the teddy doesn't do me any good. I can't take the teddy into a basketball game with me. And I can't smuggle him into school when I have to say a poem I've memorized. But, for example, I had to be one of the wise men in the Christmas pageant last year and sing a song, and all that jazz. I hid the teddy in this box of frankincense I was supposed to be carrying. I did my song perfectly; I was a big hit.

Or there was the time when I had to go up

on the stage in assembly and make a speech about how much Mrs. Creepy had done for the school, and how much we were going to miss her, and a lot of other lies that my English teacher wrote out for me. I wrapped the teddy up in some newspaper, and during rehearsal I left him on a table offstage where I could see him when I looked around. I know it's a terrible thing for a kid as big as me to go around carrying a teddy bear. It's a weakness, and it's embarrassing to me all the time. I would hate for people to find out about it. But there's nothing I can do. You know how it is with people who want to stop smoking cigarettes but can't. They have a tobacco habit. Well, I have a teddy bear habit.

Suddenly the stage door slammed open again and I went into a state of shock. The next thing I knew I was standing among a mess of dusty ropes and heavy electrical wires, looking out toward the stage. The kid with the green shoes was finishing his song. His face wasn't very green anymore. He was singing good and loud, and I could tell how happy he was feeling that he'd made it to the end.

He finished. Somewhere out front a man's voice said, "Thank you," which is what they say when you've flunked. It didn't bother Green Shoes a bit; he was just happy to have it over with. He jumped off the stage, grinning, and went out the front of the theater, and I hated him for being so happy when I was just about to be electrocuted and drowned and beheaded and tortured to death.

"Go on, boy," the old man said. My legs went weak, and I stumbled over an electric line I couldn't see in the dark. I trotted out onto the stage and looked around. There were the usual dozen people lounging around on the front rows of the theater seats. The house lights were on, and I could see how bored they were with listening to a lot of kids sing. A woman with her hair tied up behind her head and a clipboard in her hand stood up. "This is George Stable," she announced to the men lounging on the chairs. "George is twelve years old, and he has no previous experience. All right, George."

I stepped forward the way Mr. Smythe-Jones had taught me and opened my mouth, hoping that music would come out, not coconut.

"What's with the paper bag, George?" one of the men said.

I'd forgotten. I was still holding the teddy bear. I began to go all hot. "Oh," I said. "I forgot. It's just my sneakers."

"Well, let's get rid of the sneakers, George," the man said. My throat had clogged up. I couldn't speak, I couldn't swallow, so I said nothing and walked over to the side of the stage. There was a chair there, behind the curtain just out of sight of the audience. I set the bag down on the chair, where I would be able to see it, and walked back onto the stage.

I spread my arms out wide, the way Mr. Smythe-Jones had taught me, opened my mouth, and darned if I didn't actually begin to sing. It was the teddy. I wasn't singing very well, mind you, not the way I could when I was up in Mr. Smythe-Jones's studio, listening to the radiator thump and smelling Mr. Smythe-Jones's mint-flavored Life Savers. Still, it was going along all right. At first I wasn't being too expressive, the way Mr. Smythe-Jones was always yammering at me to be, but I took a quick look over at the teddy, and as I got into the song I began to feel better and better. I started feeling and seeing things again. I glanced down at the men in the first row. They were really listening to me. All at once I could tell from the way they were paying attention that it wasn't just a matter of getting through it: I had a chance for one of the parts.

Knowing that shook me a little, the way the feeling of winning always did. To keep my confidence, I turned my head a bit to take a quick glance at the teddy.

The old man with the brown banana face was sitting on the chair. The paper bag with the teddy in it had disappeared. I went cold, and my voice began to fade. I looked back out front, and went on singing. My voice was getting weak and a little rusty, and I was beginning to sweat.

Maybe the old man had put the paper bag somewhere where I could see it. I took another fast peek.

It wasn't anywhere in sight. My voice got weaker, and I knew right then I was going to mess it up. I started telling myself that I could do it, that the teddy didn't matter; then I realized I had skipped a whole part of the song. I stopped.

"Take it from the bridge, George," somebody said.

"I—my—" I said.

"Take it easy, George. Try again."

I nodded and swallowed and somehow I got going again. My voice sounded like somebody raking dead leaves off a gravel walk. I sang flat half the time and sharp the other half, and by the time I got down near the end of the song, I was going so fast that I got half the words wrong. It didn't much matter. When I finished, I didn't even wait for the man to say, "Thank you." I just walked off the stage.

The old man was headed out for the alley to haul in the next victim. "I put your lunch up on the shelf there, bub," he said, pointing. "You oughtta be more careful. I almost sat down on it."

I grabbed the paper bag and ran.

CHAPTER TWO

I LIVE ON Manhattan Island, which is the most famous part of New York City. Manhattan is where Times Square is, and Radio City Music Hall, and the Empire State Building, and Wall Street, and the stage shows, and all that jazz.

Greenwich Village, where I live, is what they call the Bohemian section of the city. A Bohemian section is where the artists hang out—painters, writers, poets, composers, and so forth. Besides the artists and writers, there are usually a lot of weirdos in a Bohemian section. In Greenwich Village we have plenty of weirdos and beatniks and dope addicts and various other kinds of nuts, like men who wear pirate scarves and beards and earrings, and women who paint their faces white and dress like little girls.

According to Pop, that's the way it always is in Bohemian sections. Anyplace you find artists, you find the screwballs. A lot of cities have Bohemian sections, but Greenwich Village is the most famous of them. I'm not saying that just to brag about where I live. It's really true. Pop and I live on West Fourth Street, a few doors west of Sixth Avenue. Greenwich Village is a mixed-up place. Some of the streets are very fancy, with trees along the sidewalks and classy buildings. Other parts are slummy: bags of garbage in the streets, bums loitering around, tattered signs in the candy-store windows. Our neighborhood is in between. The buildings are all five or six stories high and made of brick that was dirty when Washington was president and haven't gotten any cleaner since. Some of the stores along the street sell handmade jewelry and expensive sweaters and baskets and all that junk to the tourists who come down to the Village to see the beatniks. But there are regular stores, too: a grocery and a delicatessen and a meat market and a candy store. Of course over on Sixth Avenue there's a supermarket and a Rexall and a dime store. Pop and I usually go out on Saturday mornings to stock up for the week. We go to the supermarket for hamburger and spaghetti, which are a regular feature of our meals, and then around to the Rexall for toothpaste and Pop's pipe tobacco, and then to the shoe store or the dime store or whatever. Then we stop at Crespino's, a lunch counter up the street from us, and I get an egg cream while Pop has coffee and reads the paper.

We live on the fourth floor. There's no elevator; you walk up. Pop says don't complain, the exercise is good for you, but I notice that when he wants a newspaper or something he sends me down for it.

Our apartment has three rooms: a small

bedroom for me, where I have a table to do my homework on, a kitchen, and a living room with a daybed for Pop to sleep on. Actually it's not so crowded as it sounds. The living room is pretty good-sized. Pop uses about half of it for his easel and his drawing table and his taboret and the rest of the stuff he needs for his work. That half of the room is a mess most of the time. Pop is pretty sloppy in general, and he's especially sloppy with his painting stuff. Half the caps to his tubes of paint are missing, and his brushes are just as likely to be rolling around on the floor as on the taboret.

The other half of the room is our living room. We have a terrific hi-fi and almost two hundred records. I know, because I counted them once when I was home sick, lying on Pop's daybed. Then there are pictures. Man, do we have pictures. They cover practically the whole walls. There are some big ones that Pop painted, and some little ones by famous artists I never heard of. There's a charcoal drawing of my mother Pop made a long time ago. There are some copies of Old Masters, and there are one or two by friends of Pop's hidden away in dark corners. Pop is what you call an action painter. An action painter doesn't paint pictures of things. He paints the inside of his soul. Sometimes an action painter will lie his canvas down on the floor and drip paint on it straight out of the tube. Or he leans the canvas up against a wall and flings blobs of paint at it with his hands. I heard of one guy who put paint on the wheels of a kid's tricycle and rode around on the canvas. Pop has a lot of different things he does, but the main way he makes his pictures is to flip paint onto the canvas with a spoon, the way you shoot peas at kids in the school cafeteria when nobody is looking.

Except that Pop expects people to look— someday. "You might just as well face it now, Georgie, nobody gives a hoot about you until you're dead. Look at Jackson Pollock.

So I said, "Who wants to look at Jackson

Pollock if he's dead?"

Which was a mistake, because Pop said, "Okay wise guy, just for that remark, you get to spend the afternoon looking at some Pollocks." So we had to go up to the Modern Museum and look at a lot of stuff, which wasn't any different from what we had at home. Although I got even in the end. Pop took me to the museum cafeteria, and I ordered a fancy banana split, which cost a buck.

I hate to say it about my own pop, but frankly, I think the whole thing is a lot of baloney. Sure, a lot of the pictures are colorful, and if you squint your eyes right you can sometimes make out curse words, but the pictures don't give me a feeling or anything. I mean what the heck, what kind of a grown man goes around snapping paint with a spoon?

Actually, Pop is an action painter only a small part of the time. The rest of the time he's a comic-book artist. He makes up the stories, too. He works for *Smash Comics*. Sometimes he has to go up to *Smash Comics*'s offices and work there, but most of the time he works at home. He has three or four different comics that he works on, but his main one is Amorpho Man. Amorpho Man is really scientist Scott Fletcher. Scott Fletcher has the ability to turn himself into "a thick, viscuous material," sort of like molasses. The material has a special property that allows it to flow under doors, or up walls, or to seep through the ground into some caves where a lot of guys with eyes on the ends of their tentacles are plotting to destroy the planet Earth. When Amorpho Man flows over them, they get stuck in him, and he can flow them up to the National Guard or the cops or something.

The one of Pop's comics I like best, though, is his new one called Garbage Man. Garbage Man is really "mild-mannered Rick Martin, copywriter for an important advertising firm." Mostly, Rick Martin goes humming around in this cool Jaguar, making out with girls and working for his advertising agency, but when trouble impends he turns into Garbage Man, and his Jaguar turns into his trusty Garbage Truck. Garbage Man's superpower is his smell. He can beam a terrible smell in any direction he wants. It melts through walls, and it can stun people or temporarily blind them, depending on how big a shot of it Garbage Man gives them. Pop has done only a couple of issues of Garbage Man, but he thinks it might really go. I hope it does. I wouldn't mind being rich.

You would think that being an artist and living in Greenwich Village would make Pop very hip, but he isn't. The truth is, he's square, just like everybody else's old man. In fact he's worse, because as he says, "I'm trying to be a mother to you, too, Georgie." You might think that having a father for a mother would be pretty cool, but it isn't. For one thing, instead of saying, "I'm going to tell your father what you did," he already knows and takes it off your allowance. For another, if you have a father and mother who are two different people, the father can stick up for you. You know, he can say, "Leave the boy alone, Martha, he doesn't need to wear his raincoat," or whatever it is. I haven't got anyone to say "leave the boy alone, Martha." All I get is, "Don't forget to put on your raincoat," and "Did you finish your report?" and "Did you pick up your room?" Can you imagine what it's like to have your *father* take you to the dentist?

There's one more thing. Pop doesn't really make it as a mother. Sometimes he just forgets he's supposed to be a mother. For example, about half the mornings he gets up and scrambles me some eggs and tells me to clean under my fingernails and do I have my lunch money and all that jazz.

The other half of the mornings he just lies in bed and shouts out that it's late and for me to fix myself a bowl of Cocoa Puffs. Or I'll tell him two weeks ahead that I need to have sneakers and gym pants by the 24th; and when I remind him again on the 23rd he'll start bawling me out and hollering that I have to remember not to wait until the last minute to tell him these things.

But having a father for a mother has its good parts, too. He isn't always around bugging me about something, the way mothers do. A lot of the time he has to go up to *Smash Comics,* or see about some other business. Sometimes in the evenings he likes to go out to Florio's with one of his friends and have a beer. One way or another, he has to leave me on my own a lot. I have my own key to the apartment.

He was out when I got home from the *Winnie the Pooh* audition. There was a note on the kitchen table under the salt shaker, and under the note a dollar bill, just as I'd hoped. The note said, "George, back later, get some lunch at Crespino's."

I was just as glad Pop wasn't home. I was feeling pretty lousy about goofing up the audition, and I didn't much feel like answering a lot of questions. It wasn't that I minded not getting a part in the musical. That was always a long shot. I just hated thinking that I'd fallen to pieces again. I hated myself for being a loser.

I went into my room, took the teddy out of the bag, flung it up in the air, and punched it like a handball. He bounced off the wall and landed on my bed. I felt bad that I'd hit it; so I looked around to see if anyone was looking, which of course they weren't, and then I picked up the teddy and hugged it to make up for hitting it. That made me feel stupid. Finally, I shut the teddy in the top drawer of my bureau where I wasn't likely to hit it or hug it either way. Then I took off my good clothes and hung them up, and put on some dungarees and my dirty sneakers.

But I didn't go out to Crespino's for lunch. I needed that dollar bill for something else. It was going on toward two o'clock. It was getting late. I made myself a sandwich out of some leftover baked beans and ketchup, jammed the dollar into my hip pocket, and got out of there.

I was already a little bit late. Not that it mattered. Wiggsy wasn't much for being on time. Still, the truth is that he scared me a little, and I didn't like to get him mad. I peeled across Sixth Avenue against the light and down West Fourth. It was a warm day. There were a lot of people lazing up and down the sidewalk, the men with their jackets hung over one shoulder, the girls with their sweaters open. The tops on the sports cars were down, and the motorcycle cowboys lounging around on their bikes had stripped off their leather jackets and were down to their T-shirts.

When I got to Washington Square Park, I turned down MacDougal Street. MacDougal Street is more or less the hippest part of the Village. You practically don't see anybody there but beatniks with beards, the motorcycle cowboys, and the weirdos and nuts. MacDougal Street is mainly bars and coffeehouses and some little theaters and a few shops selling sandals and homemade jewelry. West Third Street runs off MacDougal; just a couple of doors down there is a shop called Wiggsy's Wig-Wam.

Wiggsy is a fantastic guitar player, but he really doesn't play very much anymore. His main business is running his store. He sells guitars and folk records and sheet music and picks and strings and junk like that. I was taking lessons in how to play rock and roll on the guitar.

I wasn't supposed to be there. Number one, Pop didn't like me hanging around with beatniks; they were a bad influence. Number two, Pop didn't like rock and roll. That was why I was studying voice with Mr. Smythe-Jones every Wednesday afternoon. The idea was to expose me to finer kinds of music. Pop had taken the fact that I had a good voice as an omen, because it saved him buying me an instrument. Number three, Pop didn't like me hanging around MacDougal Street. I guess he was afraid I'd start taking dope. He was wrong, though: nobody had ever offered me any.

Taken altogether, I could have got into a lot of trouble for taking lessons from Wiggsy, but I figured it was worth the risk. Wiggsy said that with my voice I was going to be a big star in a few years. By the time I was sixteen or seventeen, he said, I was going to be on television half the time and be chased around by autograph fans the other half.

Of course Wiggsy could just be saying that to get my two bucks every week. That was the deal: a buck a week for the lesson, and a buck a week for the secondhand guitar he was selling me. It wasn't easy raising two bucks a week without Pop knowing it. My allowance covered part of it. Another part I saved out of my lunch money by giving up desserts. I could pretty much count on Pop leaving me a dollar a week to eat at Crespino's sometime. If I got short, I borrowed from my buddy Stanky or sold something to one of the kids at school.

The trouble was that I didn't exactly trust Wiggsy. He was a good teacher and nice and all that, but he was charging me fifty dollars for the secondhand guitar he was selling me. At a dollar a week it was going to take me almost a year to pay it off. In the meantime, Wiggsy wouldn't let me take it home.

"Suppose you break it, babe?" he said. "Better to leave it with Wiggsy."

But how did I know the guitar was worth fifty dollars? How did I know the price for the guitar lessons was right? That's the trouble with being a kid: you don't know how to find out.

But I thought about the chance of being rich and famous, and I didn't ask any questions. Man, I lay awake nights thinking about it. Thinking about having a pile of loot and a Gretsch guitar and a bunch of cars scattered around hither and yon. I figured I'd have a G.T.O. uptown and a Jaguar parked in the Village, and a T-bird someplace else, so I could have a fresh car anytime I wanted. And then there'd be _Life_ photographers hanging around all the time, asking me how I got successful, and Dave Clark calling me buddy and all that. I'd buy Pop a couple of ten-thousand-dollar Jackson Pollock paintings just to show him I wasn't stuck up or anything, and still liked him.

When I went in, there was another fellow there with Wiggsy. Wiggsy does most of his business at night, when the folk singers and tourists and such are around. That's why he can give lessons in the afternoons. Wiggsy's shop is pretty small. There are music and record racks along the walls, a few guitars hanging up, and a glass counter down at the back where Wiggsy sits on a high stool. The three of us pretty much filled the shop up.

Wiggsy takes up a lot of room, anyway. He's fat. The truth is, he's very fat. He has an enormous belly and a big black beard and he dresses very cool: blue jeans and sandals and various weird kinds of shirts, and maybe a Chinese hat or an Egyptian fez or something on his head. This day he was wearing a fez and a red silk shirt with a big dragon woven into the front, which spread over most of Wiggsy's huge belly.

"You're late, babe," he said when I came in. He looked at his watch. "I ain't got time now."

I could tell that it was just an excuse to get rid of me so he could talk to the man. "Gee, I'm sorry," I said, trying to think of an explanation. I leaned back against the music racks in a casual way, and crossed my arms. "I had to audition for a Broadway show this morning and I got held up.

Wiggsy said, "Ummm. You puttin' me on, babe?"

"It's true," I said. The music rack was beginning to dig into my back, but I'd gotten everybody's attention, and I didn't want to spoil my casual pose. "It's a musical comedy about Winnie the Pooh, and they need a bunch of kids."

Wiggsy leaned over the glass display counter full of guitar strings and picks. He took a cigarette out of his beard, where he usually kept some and said, "How'd you make out?"

I wasn't about to tell the truth; on the other hand I didn't want to tell a straight lie. "Well, it's hard to tell if they like you or not." The music rack felt like it had cut clear through to my backbone, but I'd got the casual pose just right and I hated to give it up. "There wasn't much chance I'd get any of the big parts," I said, feeling behind my back to see if I was actually bleeding. "I haven't had too much experience. Right from the beginning Mr. Smythe-Jones said that the most I could hope for was a part as one of Rabbit's Friends and Relations."

I was pleased with the way I had done it. I hadn't exactly told the truth, but I hadn't told a real lie, either. In the end, it left me looking successful but modest. It isn't often that you can hit it right down the middle like that.

Wiggsy's pal had a little brown mustache and a Florida suntan he'd gotten from a sunlamp at the YMCA. He was wearing a tweedy gray sports jacket with leather buttons and a pair of black loafers. He looked pretty sharp. He was music biz, I was pretty sure. Between hanging around Wiggsy's and going up to Mr. Smythe-Jones's studio on Fifty-sixth Street behind Carnegie Hall I got so I could tell people from the music business. This guy looked like he might be a songwriter or a disc jockey or something like that.

He gave me a look. "Exactly what experience have you had, fella?" He leaned back against Wiggsy's glass counter in a pose that had me out-casualed. Then he dealt a gold cigarette lighter out of his pocket like a magician pulling a card out of his sleeve. Man, was he smooth. He lit Wiggsy's cigarette without even looking at him, and then the lighter disappeared like magic.

"My experience?" I said.

"Yeah. You said you hadn't had *much* experience. That means you just have had some, eh fella?"

It just goes to show that you ought to prac-tice your lies at home before you show them off in public. I didn't know what to say. I didn't want to backtrack in front of anyone who could flip a cigarette lighter around like that, but on the other hand I didn't want to get caught in a bigger lie, either. To give me time to think of something, I stalled by undoing my belt buckle and doing it up again as if it were too tight or too loose, and then I said, "Well, you know, it isn't much. Mostly these recitals Mr. Smythe-Jones puts on for the parents and stuff."

It sounded flat and not very impressive at all. I remembered that one of Mr. Smythe-Jones' older students had once gone on a radio show called "The Young People's Concerts." It wasn't hard to remember. Mr. Smythe-Jones had gone around for weeks afterward saying, "Brilliant young singer on 'The Young People's Concerts' the other day, one of my students, don't chew know." I tried to slip my hand in behind my back to ease the pain. "We used to do 'The

Young People's Concerts' sometimes," I said. That sounded *too* impressive. "I mean we did it a couple of times." Music Biz looked amused. "How many times, fella? Twice? Once?"

I decided to tell the smallest possible lie. "Well, once," I said.

"I thought it was probably something like that," he said. "What did you sing?"

For a moment I had a strong impulse to blurt out that I was kidding, that it hadn't happened at all; but I didn't. "Without a Song" didn't seem right for "The Young People's Concert." "'The Donkey Serenade,'" I said, which was another song I'd studied with Mr. Smythe-Jones.

Wiggsy was giving me a funny look. I could tell he was trying to decide whether I was lying. "When did all this happen, babe?" He took a pack of cigarettes out of his shirt pocket and began sticking them one by one into his beard, where he could get them later. "I don't remember anything about it."

I began to sweat. Wiggsy was going to grill me. "Before I started taking guitar with you, it was. A while ago. I forget the exact date."

"Yeah, babe?" Wiggsy said.

But Music Biz saved me. "You take guitar from Wiggsy? And study voice?"

The music rack had sawed halfway through my spinal column, and I decided I'd better give up the casual pose before I fainted from the agony. I straightened, and felt around my back for blood. "I'll be honest," I said, which was a nice change. "My Pop wants me to study classical, but what I really like is rock and roll. I study voice with this Mr. Smythe-Jones on Wednesday, and I take guitar from Wiggsy on Saturday." I almost made a mistake and blurted out that Pop didn't know anything about Wiggsy or the guitar lessons, but I stopped myself just in time. I was afraid Wiggsy would make me quit if he found out. "Can you read music, fella?" Music Biz asked.

"Sure. Some. If it's not too hard."

"Is he any good, Wiggsy?"

Turnabout was fair play. For weeks Wiggsy had been telling me what a genius I was on the guitar and how famous I was going to be, and now he was stuck with it whether he believed it or not. "I been showing him some chords," he said. "He blows pretty good. I mean he's no Django Reinhart, but he can bang out the easy changes pretty good."

Music Biz reached into his pocket and flipped out a card the same way he'd magicked up the cigarette lighter. "Listen fella," he said, "maybe I can use you. Have your pop give me a horn on Monday." He handed me the card and slapped Wiggsy on the shoulder. "I've got to split."

I stared at the little white card in my hand. It said:

> *Thomas Woodward*
> WOODWARD AND HAYES
> *Television Productions*
> AL5-9210

CHAPTER THREE

HERE WERE about twelve things wrong with the whole idea. In the first place, Pop hated television, just like he hated rock and roll, and egg creams, and ugly stickers, and anything else that I liked. In fact, he hated it so much that we didn't even have a television set. Every once in a while I'd ask, please couldn't we get one. He always said the same thing: television was for mental defectives, and besides, he was damned if he was going to pay good money just so the National Association of Manufacturers could brainwash his son. My opinion was that it was a free country, and I ought to be allowed to get brainwashed if I wanted, but my opinion was

wrong, because if you've got an old man like Pop, it isn't a free country. So that was one thing wrong with the idea.

The second thing wrong with it was that even if Pop was willing to call up this guy, first I'd have to tell him all about Wiggsy and using my lunch money for guitar lessons and all that jazz. Man, it wouldn't be worth it. I just wasn't ready to be starved and tortured and have my allowance cut off for forty or fifty years. So that was another thing wrong with the idea.

The third thing wrong with it was my problem. Of course I didn't know exactly what kind of thing this guy Thomas Woodward had in mind, but for sure it didn't have anything to do with teddy bears. I mean, you can't go out to sing rock and roll on television holding a teddy bear in your arms. It wouldn't be just the show, either. There'd be auditions and rehearsals and all that jazz, too. It would be just too embarrassing to admit that I had a teddy bear habit. I'd have to figure out some way to sneak the teddy into all of them. I mean maybe there might be some way I could hide it behind a camera. Or maybe I could pretend it was some kind of hip joke. Or pretend I'd just got it for my kid brother. No, it was too complicated. You could get away with some kind of stunt like that once or twice, but you'd never get away with it day after day.

So there were twelve reasons against the whole thing; but still, I couldn't get over the idea. At school on Monday, I couldn't do anything but think about it. I could see Ed Sullivan saying, "All right kids, here's what you've been waiting for, the new teenage singing sensation, Georgie Stable." (I figured I would be thirteen by then.) And the kids in the audience screaming and fainting from the agony, and me out there in snazzy black motorcycle boots and a gold silk jacket and a Gretsch guitar. Man, it was so delicious that I shuddered right there in school, and made Miss Hornet ask sarcastically if I was coming down with a cold. Still, there wasn't anything I could do about it. After school, I walked down Sixth Avenue, taking the card out of my pocket to look at it, and putting it back, and taking it out again. Then I went around to Crespino's and sat there, drinking an egg cream and looking at it some more. Looking at it didn't make anything happen. I looked up at the sign Mr. Crespino had chalked on his blackboard: TODAY STEW 50¢. That didn't make anything happen, either. So I went home. Pop was working at his drawing table. I went into my bedroom and flung the card into my bureau drawer under the teddy. I felt itchy and cross and sore at Pop for being against television and so forth. I flopped down on the daybed in the living room and turned on some rock and roll on the hi-fi as loud as I dared, just to annoy Pop.

Pop was staring at his drawing board, his chin in his hands. There was a cup of cold coffee on the taboret. He'd slopped about half of it on his paintbrushes, and there were about four hundred cigarette butts in his ashtray, and I knew he was having trouble getting an idea.

"Turn that darn thing down," he said. "I'm trying to concentrate."

I didn't answer him, but I turned it down.

"I'm trying to think up a new enemy for Garbage Man. I'm tired of those same old Mars men."

I rolled over on my back and stared up at the ceiling.

"Why don't you have him captured by a couple of rock-and-roll singers?" I said as crossly as I dared. "In the end he could smell them to death. That ought to make you happy."

"Hmmm," he said. "Rock-and-roll singers. Not bad. A good angle. The contemporary touch." He completely missed the idea that I was sore at him. He slapped his hand down on his drawing board, and then he got up and began pacing around the room the way he does when he gets an idea, talking to himself.

"Let's suppose the invaders from the alien

world come down to knock off the planet Earth. They're odd looking, and we suppose they see the necessity of disguising themselves as Earth men until they can conclude their nefarious plans. We suppose that they have—what?"

"Stupid arms sticking out of their stupid stomachs," I said in a snotty way.

But he was concentrating on his big idea, and he didn't notice that I was being snotty. "Hmmm. Yes," he said, pacing around and around. "Arms sticking out of their stomachs. Hmmm. Yes. And naturally they need a way to hide the arms when they go out in public. Yes. Guitars. They go out in public disguised as rock-and-roll singers, using guitars to hide their electric arms."

He went back to his drawing board and flopped down in his chair. "Very good, George," he said. "You've been a big help."

Trying to annoy him I'd done him a favor. It just shows about being a loser. I stomped off to my room.

"What's bugging you?" he said. I slammed the door and he went back to work. And then, because I was sore, I took the little card out of the bureau drawer, tore it into tiny pieces, and dropped them out of the window down the air shaft. As I watched them go, I got a sick feeling, sick and sorry that I'd done it. But I'm a loser, and it was too late to be sorry. So I went up to the Y and got into a basketball game. I was so mad at myself for destroying my big opportunity that I was the terror of the court—at least until I stopped being sore at myself.

For the next few days I felt sort of lousy in a calm way. I didn't care about doing anything especially. Because of that I got a good start on my science project, which left me pretty free all weekend. It just goes to show that a little good always comes out of everything. My philosophy is that there's an advantage to everything, if you think about it. For example, there's even something good about falling off the Empire State Building: you have a fabulous experience on the way down.

During that week I decided to quit guitar. The good thing to come out of that was that I would get back the seventeen dollars I had paid on the guitar. There wasn't any point in going on with guitar lessons as far as I could see. I mean between Pop hating rock and roll and me being a loser, there wasn't much chance that I'd ever get to be a big hero. It made me despair just to think about it.

So I thought about the seventeen dollars instead. Of course I couldn't get back the seventeen dollars I'd paid him for lessons; that was gone. But the seventeen I'd paid toward the guitar was mine. At the beginning, Wiggsy had said, "If you decide to quit, babe, you get your money back."

Seventeen dollars was a pretty big chunk of money. For a long time I'd wanted a radio of my own for my room, so that Pop wouldn't always be telling me to turn that darn thing down. I knew I could get a pretty good table model for about fifteen bucks at a discount store up on

Fourteenth Street. That would leave me a couple of dollars to blow on egg creams—almost two weeks of egg creams at fifteen cents a piece. Of course, I *could* put the seventeen dollars in my savings account, but it wasn't very likely that I would. I'm not that much of a loser.

Buying an important possession like a radio is something you take a friend along on, so Saturday morning I called up my buddy, Everett Stanky.

"I'm going to buy a radio," I said, "but I can't buy it until this after."

"Why not?"

"I'll tell you later. Meet me over at the checker players at one o'clock."

In one corner of Washington Square Park are some little tables with checkerboards built into the tops. The men play checkers or chess there, and there are usually a bunch of people standing around watching them. It was where Stanky and I usually met.

Stanky is about my height, but he is very

skinny and weak-looking. Stanky is the type you take for a sissy. He wears glasses, and he has black hair falling over his forehead, and he throws like a girl, and his skin is so tender he could cut himself on a lollipop. On top of it, there's his name. He doesn't want people to call him Everett, naturally, so they end up calling him Stinky. Stinky Stanky. Except me. I call him Stanky.

But even though he throws like a girl, Stanky is no loser. There are four things he can do. Number one, he can beat anyone in the neighborhood at Ping-Pong. Number two, he can play a whole lot of études and preludes and stuff on the piano. They always make him play the "Star Spangled Banner" for assemblies. Number three, he gets straight As. Number four, he can bottom deal a pack of cards. It's amazing to watch him; you can't see him do it, his hands go so fast.

Stanky had a bag of mixed nuts he had swiped. "They went out to the theater last night. They're not awake yet. I found it on the coffee table."

We walked around the park, sharing out the nuts. In New York October is sometimes as warm as summer. There were bums sleeping on the park benches. Some of them were bandaged where they'd got into fights. Some students from New York University were sitting around on the grass with their books, pretending to study but really trying to make out with the girls. Some people were walking their dogs, and over near the big fountain in the middle of the park a couple of beatniks were playing Frisbee. They were playing with one hand because they each had a can of beer in the other. The beer kept slopping all over the place when they threw the Frisbee. We just walked around looking at things, eating the nuts, and scaring up bursts of pigeons; and I told Stanky about it.

"Pop wouldn't let me do it in a million years, man. In the first place. In the second place, he'd give me a shot in the head if he found out about Wiggsy."

Stanky held out the nut bag. I reached in and got the biggest one I could grab, a huge almond. "Sorry about that," I said.

"What are you going to tell Wiggsy if you quit?" he asked.

"I don't know. Maybe I'll tell him Pop won't let me any more."

"It would be the truth." He dumped the last few nuts out of the bag into his hand. "Sorry about that," he said.

I grabbed the nuts out of his hand and tossed them into my mouth. "Sorry about that," I said.

He grabbed my sleeve and gave me a shot in the arm. "Sorry about that," he said.

I grabbed his sleeve. "Sorry about—"

"You can't hit me. I'm wearing glasses," he said.

We quit horsing around. "I don't know what to do."

"Well."

"What do you think I ought to do, Stank?" Suddenly I realized that I hoped he would talk me out of quitting the guitar. The truth was that I didn't want to quit. The truth was that I wanted to call this television guy, get on some program, and become a big star with a lot of autograph fans following me around everywhere I went. But I didn't want to admit to Stanky that I'd changed my mind. I mean I had made my decision, and it would seem weak and wishy-washy of me to keep changing my mind all the time. It was a silly way to be, but it was the way I felt. Somebody had to talk me out of quitting.

But Stanky didn't do it. Instead he said, "Let's walk down to Wiggsy's and get the loot."

So we did. Wiggsy was sitting up on his stool behind the glass counter at the end of his store. He was wearing a red Egyptian fez and a purple silk shirt with yellow glass buttons, and he was drinking a can of beer. It seemed like everybody in the Village was drinking a can of beer. Wiggsy's stomach was so fat he could use it for a table to rest his beer can on.

"What are you two cats doing for jollies this morning?" he said, trying to put on that he was the friendly type.

I shrugged. "Nothing. Just messing around." I began trying to think of some way to get Wiggsy to talk me out of quitting my lessons. I was afraid he was too cool for that. On top of it, I was beginning to be worried about asking Wiggsy for my money back. "We were just up at the park chasing pigeons," I said.

"Yeah," Wiggsy said.

Nobody said anything for a minute. Wiggsy picked up a pack of cigarettes from the glass counter, shook out four or five, and began tucking them into his beard. Stanky began looking at some sheet music to pretend he didn't know I was scared to ask for my money back. I undid my belt buckle and buckled it up again.

"Yeah," Wiggsy said. He had got all of the cigarettes stowed into his beard, and now he took one out, put it in his mouth, and struck a match.

I blurted out, "Wiggsy, I'm thinking about quitting the guitar."

He was very cool. He held the match to the cigarette and puffed out a stream of smoke. "I don't know why you want to do that for, babe."

I felt better. Maybe he would talk me out of it after all. Still, I had to argue with him a little, for the show. "Well, my father doesn't want me to take any more."

He kept his cool. "Well, all right babe, if that's the way it is."

I got red and prickly. "I mean, maybe I could talk him out of it."

He sucked on his cigarette. "I don't know, babe. If he don't want you to maybe you'd better not."

I was stuck for anything to say next. Wiggsy began fooling around with some sheet music he had on the counter. I waited for him to

say something like, "Why don't you talk to
him?" or something, but he just went on fooling
around with the sheet music. Then I began
waiting for him to say something like, "Here's
your seventeen dollars back," and then after a
while I realized he wasn't going to say that
either. I was going to have to say it.

"I don't need the seventeen dollars right
away," I said. I got red again.

Wiggsy looked up and began shooting out
little spurts of cigarette smoke. "Well, babe, I
kind of hate to see you quit when you were coming along so groovy. I don't say you were any
Segovia, mind you, but you were getting there,
babe."

Now was my big chance to keep my mouth
shut, but of course that wasn't very likely.
"Well, I don't know, Wiggsy," I said.

He leaned his elbows on the counter, which
wasn't easy, considering how fat he was. "Say,
did you call up that fella, babe? The one who
was in here the other day?"

I blushed again because of what I had done with the man's card. "I was going to, but I lost his address," I said.

"Well listen, babe, I wouldn't kid you. He called me up yesterday. He wanted to know what was with you."

I didn't think that was true, but I decided to believe it anyway. "No kidding?" I said.

"Sure babe. This is no time to quit. You got it made."

"Well, I don't know," I said.

"Give him a horn. Woodward and Hayes. Look them up in the phone book." He dumped the last of the beer down his throat, slid off the stool, put one arm around me and one around Stanky, and began pushing us toward the door. "Give him a horn, babe. Now you two cats scram. I got work to do." And he shoved us out into the street.

So there I was. I didn't have the money, and I wasn't really talked into doing anything about that show.

Stanky waited until Wiggsy shut the door to his shop and then he nudged me and said, "Sorry about that."

"Well, what did you expect me to do," I said crossly.

"I didn't do anything. Don't get sore at me."

We walked up the street a way and then we stopped and leaned on a new Buick that was parked there. I was confused and sore, and I began twanging the car aerial to get even. "There goes seventeen bucks," I said.

Stanky took off his glasses and twirled them around by one of the hooks. "Well, if you ask me, you ought to call up that guy."

"Don't be dumb. I can't. My father has to call. They have to get his permission. Stop swinging your glasses. You're making me nervous."

Stanky leaned up against the Buick. "Sorry about that," he said. "Stop twanging that aerial."

"Sorry about that," I said.

"You know what you ought to do, Georgie?

You ought to get Mr. Smythe-Jones to call the guy up."

"Smythe-Jones? Aw come on." But the minute he'd said it a cold chill had gone up my spine. And I knew he was right. Mr. Smythe-Jones would love it. Afterward he would go around boasting about how he'd got one of his students on television, and what a great success he made out of everybody who studied with him, and how he had a lot of ins with television and so forth and so on. Oh, it was exactly the right idea. And it made me go cold and scared, because I knew that if I managed it right I could go on television for sure. Not just in my day-dreams, but for real.

Being as real as that, it scared me. "Yeah, Smythe-Jones," I said. "Let's go over to your house and swipe something to eat."

CHAPTER FOUR

SPENT THE next three days thinking up excuses for not getting Mr. Smythe-Jones to call up Woodward, the television producer. Thinking up excuses is something I've always been pretty good at. The big thing in thinking up excuses is to make them a little bit unbelievable. That way, people think: He couldn't have made that up, it's too unbelievable. Nobody will believe an excuse that's too believable. For example, if you tell the teacher that you didn't do your math because you forgot your book, she'll just give you a bawling out; but if you say you didn't do it because it was your grandmother's hundredth birthday and you all had to go up to

Scarsdale for the party, she'll start asking about
your grandmother and forget about the math.
Besides, if you make them a little unbelievable,
you'll get more variety into your excuses; they'll
have a professional ring you can be proud of.

Making up excuses to yourself is a whole lot
harder than making up excuses for your teacher.
I was having a lot of trouble getting myself to
believe the ones I was making to get out of asking Mr. Smythe-Jones to call the television producer. The first one I made up was that I
shouldn't worry about it until I'd finished my
science report, so as not to be distracted. The
trouble was that my science report was almost
finished, so that excuse didn't work. Then I
decided that I ought to wait until I'd had a couple of more lessons from Wiggsy; but I knew
that a couple of more lessons weren't going to
make much difference one way or another. So
that excuse wasn't any good, either. Then I
decided that the whole business was making me
sick and nervous and was giving me a cold, and

that it would be smarter to wait until I felt better; but, of course, the longer I waited the sicker I'd get, so that excuse flunked out, too.

I should have known better than to get started on my excuses so far in advance. By the time I got onto the Sixth Avenue Subway to go up to Mr. Smythe-Jones's for my vocal lesson, I'd used up all the good ones, and was down to deciding that maybe Mr. Woodward was a Mars man and the whole thing was a plot to kidnap me. When I got off the subway at the Seventh Avenue stop, I'd used up all the lousy ones, too. The only excuse I had left was that I was just plain scared. For me, being scared isn't much of an excuse: too believable.

Mr. Smythe-Jones's studio is on Fifty-sixth Street facing the back of Carnegie Hall. Carnegie Hall is about the most famous concert hall in the United States, I guess, and Mr. Smythe-Jones liked to give everybody the idea that he used to sing there a lot. He went around saying things like, "When I was singing at

Carnegie," but the truth is that he only sang there once, as part of a hundred-voice choir. I know, because one day when he was busy buttering up the mother of some snotty kid who didn't want to learn how to sing either, I went through his scrapbook and found the program.

Mr. Smythe-Jones had his studio in his apartment. There was the front room, which was really a regular living room with thousands of photographs of opera stars and conductors and dancers and actors hanging on the walls. And there was the back room, which had in it only a beat-up Steinway practice piano, a metronome, some shelves full of old music, a blackboard, a huge rubber plant almost as high as the ceiling, and a terrible smell of chalk and mint-flavored Life Savers mixed up together.

When I got there, Mr. Smythe-Jones was sitting in the studio drinking a cup of tea. He was never much more in favor of listening to me sing "The Donkey Serenade" fifty times over and over again than I was in singing it. He was always willing to waste some time talking something or other over, provided that he didn't get the idea you were just stalling. If he thought you were stalling, he'd say something like, "George, your father isn't paying me good money to listen to you chatter, don't chew know." Then he'd make you work twice as hard and keep you ten minutes over. Still, if you were smart about it, you could stall. For example, some kids would wait until they came to the hard part and then they'd start in with some line like, "Say, Mr. Smythe-Jones, who do you think was best, Mario Lanza or Ezio Pinza?" Of course Mr. Smythe-Jones would smell a rat and say, "We'll discuss that after the lesson, don't chew know."

The smart thing to do was to start your stall during the *easy* part, so as not to arouse his sus-picions. On this particular day he was teaching me some aria written by somebody whose name I couldn't pronounce. It had a hard section just after the middle, and I knew that easy place after that was where I should stop and ask him for help on the television thing. But I didn't. We kept going over the song and over it, and every time I'd finish up that hard part and come to a natural stopping place where I could have spoken up, my mouth froze and nothing came out. The chance would pass, and Smythe-Jones would start me up again, and off I'd go. So the time went along, and all of a sudden the lesson was over, and Mr. Smythe-Jones was saying, "Top hole, Georgie," or some other lie. I knew that if I didn't say something right then I never would, and I'd go home and commit suicide and hate myself all the rest of my life.

So I blurted out, "Mr. Smythe-Jones, I have to ask your advice on something."

"Oh yes, Georgie?" He fished out a dirty, crumpled end of a Life Saver pack, sat down on the piano bench, crossed his legs, and got ready to listen. If there was anything Mr. Smythe-Jones liked, it was to have his advice asked about something. He worked a mint-flavored

Life Saver out of the pack. "Yes, tell me about it, George."

"The thing is this," I said. "I happened to meet up with a television producer, and he wants me to call him up about some kind of show or something."

First, Smythe-Jones pursed his lips, then he raised his eyes, and then he popped the Life Saver into his mouth, and I knew he was trying to decide whether he ought to get sore because he hadn't been consulted in the beginning, or pleased because one of his students might do something he could boast about for a year afterward.

Finally he said, "I don't like the sound of it, George. Who is this man?"

I had written the name and phone number down on a piece of scratch paper, and I took it out and handed it to him. "Mr. Woodward. Of Woodward and Hayes."

Smythe-Jones shook his head slowly, and began turning the Life Saver over and over in his mouth with his tongue. "Cahn't say that I know them, George," he said in a slow, serious way that meant that they were probably liars and cheaters. Smythe-Jones thought that everybody in the world he didn't know personally were liars and cheaters.

So I looked back at him very seriously and I said, "Well, that's what Pop was wondering about. He doesn't know anything about the television and all, and he thought maybe you might call them up and see if there was anything wrong with it."

I figured I was on safe ground. Getting one of his students on television, or written up somewhere made him hum like a bee. If the thing worked out he could go around for months afterward saying, "Didn't happen to see the *Telephone Hour* lahst night, by chance? Student of mine on it, don't chew know. Virtually tone deaf when he came to me, don't chew know. Hardly believe it myself, don't chew know." And then of course it would give him a great thing to say when he was trying to persuade mothers to send their snotty kids to him for lessons. "Get a little telly for my students from time to time. Cahn't promise anything, but one cahn't tell, don't chew know."

He stopped turning the Life Saver over and tucked it away in his cheek. "Well, George," he said slowly.

"Pop would sure appreciate it."

"Yes," he said, "I can understand that. Life Saver, George?" He held out the pack, but the pack looked so crumpled and dirty I figured I might get ptomaine poisoning and said no thank you.

"I suppose I'd better do something about it," he said. "Wouldn't want to have one of my students mixed up in some tasteless little affair. Wouldn't look right, don't chew know. Bad show, that sort of thing."

He got up and went out into his living room, where the telephone was, and I sat down on the piano bench and waited, feeling nervous.

I could hear him dial, and after a bit I could hear him explaining to Mr. Woodward what it was all about. "Boy's voice teacher. Father ahsked me to take commahnd, so to speak. Ha, ha. Don't have the picture, quite . . . Righto . . . Right chew are . . . Quite. . . . Glad to help out, mind . . ."

For about five minutes he went dribbling on this way, don't chew knowing and righto-ing. Then he hung up and came out and told me that they were holding auditions at four o'clock on Friday, and he'd take me up. And naturally, right after he told me that my legs began to get weak and shaky, and my heart to go ripping along full speed, and my stomach to fill up with cold marbles. But there was nothing I could do about that.

That was Wednesday. I had only two days to get ready. In a way that was lucky. Between being nervous about the audition, and excited about the chance of becoming rich and famous, and scared about being caught by Pop, I could hardly eat anything during meals. If the audition had been a couple of weeks away, say, I'd have died of starvation before I got to it.

The first thing I did was to talk Wiggsy into lending me my guitar. He didn't like the idea very much, but since he'd been pushing the thing he had to go along. Of course I couldn't keep it at my place. Thursday afternoon I walked down with Stanky and got it, and we took it up to his place and hid it in his bedroom.

The Stankys are pretty rich. Well-to-do, I guess you'd call it. Mr. Stanky is some kind of a public relations man or something. He makes a pile of loot. They live in a private house on Eleventh Street, which has trees along the sidewalk and is very fancy. He likes to think he is very hip because he owns a couple of action paintings and is always listening to a lot of scratchy old jazz records that were made when Washington was president. The truth is that he isn't any more hip than my pop. Less, even: at least Pop isn't well-to-do.

Anyway, it wasn't likely that the Stankys would care if I left the guitar there, but just to be safe, we hid it up on Stanky's closet shelf behind a box of old sweaters and stuff. So that took care of one problem.

The other problem Stanky couldn't help me on, because even Stanky didn't know that I had a teddy bear habit. I knew perfectly well that if I went up to the audition without the teddy I'd panic and start fainting all over the place and embarrass Mr. Smythe-Jones and feel ashamed and hate myself for about two weeks afterward. On the other hand, if I could manage to smuggle the teddy in I knew that at least I wouldn't start fainting. That didn't say that I'd win the audition; that's something you could never figure on. But at least I wouldn't do anything to make myself ashamed and embarrassed. And there was always the chance I'd win.

I thought of several plans. The first idea I had was to take the teddy to the audition in a shoe box. I figured I could explain that I'd just bought a brand-new pair of twelve-dollar shoes, and that I wanted them right where I could keep an eye on them because my old man would kill me if I lost them. But after I'd thought this idea over carefully, I realized that they might have some kind of cloak closet or check room, where they'd insist that I put my twelve-dollar shoes for safekeeping.

The second idea I had was to put the teddy in a little canvas bag of some kind. I'd say that I had diabetes or asthma or something, and had to carry this special medicine around with me wherever I went. Of course nobody would dare to take my medicine away from me. But then it came to me that maybe they wouldn't want anybody on television who might keel over in the middle of the show. So that idea was no good.

All day Thursday, when I was supposed to be paying attention to my teachers, I was trying to think up a hiding place for the teddy. I couldn't come up with anything. All I got for my work was a bawling out about every fifteen minutes for daydreaming. By bedtime I was getting worried. I sat down on the edge of my bed in my underwear and began to play an imaginary guitar, pretending I was at the audition to see if anything would come to me.

All at once I remembered that guitars are hollow. There's plenty of room for a teddy inside, and there's a big round hole in the middle to push him through.

I sat on the bed, thinking about it. If I loosened the strings up a good deal, I could surely push them aside far enough to squeeze the teddy through. I could push it back out of sight a little bit. It'd stick there. It was fat enough so that he wouldn't slide around. It was a perfect plan. I'd have it right where I could get a peek at him or even reach in and touch him when I began to get nervous. Nobody would know; it'd be completely hidden.

The idea tickled me so much that when Pop started shouting at me to go brush my teeth I just giggled. And I dreamed all night of being rich and famous and standing in a spotlight on a stage, wearing a gold silk jacket, blue-and-white cowboy boots, playing a brand-new Gretsch guitar, and being hollered at by a lot of crazy girls.

But the next day I was nervous all over again. I could hardly eat breakfast, and I could hardly stand being in school. During lunch hour I thought of cutting out to go someplace and shoot baskets to get over my nervousness, but I was afraid I'd get into trouble, and I didn't need trouble at that moment. So I spent the day sliding around in my seat and drumming on my desk with my pencil, until finally Miss Hornet told me to get the ants out of my pants, which made everybody laugh.

At three o'clock, Stanky and I peeled over to his place for the guitar. I was supposed to be at Woodward and Hayes at four o'clock. It didn't leave me much time to get home, stow the teddy into the guitar, and get uptown.

Stanky got the guitar out of his closet and said, "Good luck," and I said, "Yeah," and peeled out of there and down Sixth Avenue as fast as I could go, jumping all the lights. I was all in a sweat that I might meet Pop walking around the Village someplace. That's the trouble with having a father who doesn't go to a regular job; you can't count on him being out of the way when you're getting into trouble.

I got to our building without running into him. Of course I still didn't know whether he was up in the apartment, working, or had gone out someplace. I hid the guitar down behind the stairs, where they keep the baby carriages and bicycles, and charged upstairs.

Pop was working over his drawing board, smoking his pipe, and slopping cold coffee all over the place.

"Hi," he said.

"Hi," I said, zooming past him, "I gotta go."

"Whoa, boy, take it easy," he said leaning back and fumbling around among his paint tubes for his pipe. "What's the big rush? Life isn't that short."

Right away I knew I'd made a bad mistake. Parents are contradictory, and one who's two parents in one is twice as contradictory. My mistake was to come belting into the apartment like that, for that kind of thing was bound to get him going on a big philosophical lecture about how nothing is that important; people should learn to relax more and enjoy each moment as it comes.

What I should have done was to come sauntering in and start telling him some long, dull complaint about how the math teacher was always yelling at me for no reason, and how I couldn't get my science done on time because somebody stole my ballpoint pen, and so forth and so on. That would have got him to say, "You can't blame others for your own problems. You have to work some of these things out for yourself. Now don't bother me. I'm working."

But naturally I'd been stupid and come charging into the apartment full speed, and now I was in for it.

"What's the big rush?" he said.

"Stanky's waiting. We have to get up to the Hayden Planetarium before the four o'clock show." I'd have said the Museum of Modern Art, but that was *too* unbelievable.

"It won't hurt Stanky to wait." He went on fumbling for his pipe among the paints, and at last he found it and could start fumbling for his tobacco pouch. There wasn't anything I could do but stand there and wait for him to get finished. Finally, after a couple of hours he found the pouch and began filling the bowl of the pipe. "How'd school go today?" he asked.

"Okay," I said.

"Just okay?"

"It went fine."

He put the pipe in his mouth and began searching around among the paint tubes and the spilled coffee for some matches.

"I gotta go," I said. It was a stupid thing to say, but I couldn't help it; it just slipped out.

"Stanky can wait," he said. He went on looking for the matches, and after about a month he found them.

"We'll miss the show, Pop."

He opened the matchbook, tore off a match, struck it, and began sucking the flame into the pipe and casting out big puffs of smoke. He went on doing this all through December and into March, and finally around the end of June he got the pipe going and he said, "Math going all right these days? No more Fs?"

"No, fine, I got a B."

"Where's my ashtray?" he said. He put the pipe down on the edge of his taboret, where it began to go out, and looked around for his ashtray. The year ran out, and then another year, and then a couple of decades, and along about the time we were getting into the twenty-first century he found the ashtray down on the floor, where he'd put it. I looked at the pipe. It was about out, and I knew I'd faint from the agony if I had to go through that lighting scene again. I was desperate to tell him to start smoking again quick, but I didn't dare.

"Can I go now?" I said.

"Stanky can wait," he said. "How's the English going?"

"Fine, great, maybe I'll get an A," I said.

"Stop twitching like that." He picked up the pipe and gave it a suck. No smoke came out. I nearly collapsed; but he sucked a couple of times more and it began to smoke, so he went on sucking and sucking and stirring up smoke. The centuries went past, and the sun began to go out, and the earth began to grow cold, and the ice began to creep down from the polar cap, and just about the time that the last traces of life were dying out on this planet, he got the pipe going in a way to satisfy him, and he said, "Okay, you can scram. Be home in time for supper."

I had pretty nearly turned to stone, but I got my legs moving and peeled into the bedroom and grabbed the teddy. Holding him down by my leg where Pop couldn't see him, I raced out of the apartment, down the stairs, grabbed the guitar case from behind the baby carriages, and tore for the subway.

I was all in a sweat by the time a train came in and I was headed uptown, but I still had the guitar to work over. Luckily, there weren't too many people in the car that time of day; it was too embarrassing to get caught shoving a teddy into your guitar. By keeping the guitar case more or less propped up on the seat beside me I was pretty well concealed. Then all I had to do was loosen the strings, push the teddy down into the hole, and jam him back inside, where he wouldn't work loose. If he had been a human being, he'd have gotten his back scraped up badly by those strings, but that's the advantage of being a teddy bear: you don't feel things very much.

It was tough tuning the guitar on the subway, but I got close enough, I figured I'd have a chance to finish the job later.

As it worked out, I wasn't more than about

ten minutes late to meet Mr. Smythe-Jones. We began walking crosstown at a good clip, the guitar bumping and banging against my leg. "Mustn't be late, don't chew know," he said. "They don't need you; you need them." By which I took it that Mr. Smythe-Jones was as nervous as I was about the audition. Well, not quite. That wasn't possible.

The truth is that if I'd known what a big deal the whole thing was I'd have been a lot more nervous than I was. This wasn't any little kid's party. Woodward and Hayes' offices were on Madison Avenue in one of these brand-new glass buildings on stilts, which you can walk around under. Man, was it snazzy. We went up in an automatic elevator, the kind you run yourself. It was the fanciest elevator I'd ever been in. Most elevators around my neighborhood have cigarette butts on the floor and initials scratched into the paint on the walls. This one had a rug on the floor and music playing out of the ceiling.

There were plenty of rugs around on the floor at Woodward and Hayes, too. There were modern tables around with classy magazines lying on them, and vases of flowers, and a secretary dressed up as if she was going to a party.

I can tell you, it had me scared, and I got even more scared when Mr. Woodward, the fellow I'd originally met down at Wiggsy's, came out of somewhere. This time he was wearing a green tweed jacket, brown loafers, and a brown bow tie. He still had the same fake suntan, and when he walked toward us he whipped that same gold cigarette lighter out of midair like a magician and lit his cigarette. Man, was he cool. You could tell that he was a guy who would never get nervous at anything. I could see him in front of a firing squad flipping that cigarette lighter around and saying something cool like, "Tell the fellows to aim for my heart, Colonel, I hate to get my hair mussed."

It was me who was going before the firing

squad, however. Mr. Woodward made the cigarette lighter disappear, shook hands with Mr. Smythe-Jones, put his arm around my shoulder, and said, "The clan is gathering in the studio, cookie. Shall we join them?" He twiddled the lit cigarette between his fingers like a drum majorette swishing the baton through her legs. "The boy reads music pretty well, Mr. Smythe-Jones?"

Smythe-Jones nodded. "All my pupils read, Mr. Woodward. Get the fundamentals first, don't chew know. Cahn't build a house on sand, don't chew know."

He went on about fundamentals for a while, trying to impress Mr. Woodward, and at about the fifth don't chew know we reached the studio and went in.

As I found out later, it was a regular recording studio. Woodward and Hayes were mainly in the business of taping musical backgrounds and singing commercials, which they call jingles in the advertising business. For example, you know how on a detective show the good cop is always going into a nightclub and asking the bartender where Frisco hangs out? Maybe they want to have a little band in the nightclub playing some jazz or something. The people you see on the television are usually just actors pretending to play the music. The music you hear was taped in a studio by people like Woodward and Hayes. The reason for that is real musicians don't look like musicians: they're usually pudgy and red-faced and look like they ought to be train conductors or butchers. People expect musicians to be thin and have long sloppy hair and look as if they had a bad cold; so on television they use actors.

Woodward and Hayes taped background music of this kind. They made singing commercials, mostly for radio, but sometimes for television, about how great the beer and the suntan oil is. One other thing they did was to help put together musical acts. Suppose one of the big shows wanted a quartet to sing along with the star; Woodward and Hayes would choose the singers, hire somebody to write out the music, and take charge of the rehearsals. I was trying out for something like that.

Woodward and Hayes had three or four studios, but the one Mr. Woodward took us into was the biggest of them—big as a really big living room. The walls were white and there were a lot of lights in the place, so that the room looked airy and big. Scattered around were a lot of microphones and cables, and two huge grand pianos on small wheels so they could be moved around easily. Behind a huge picture window was the engineer's control room, full of knobs and panels and big tape-recording machines; and sitting in a row on folding chairs along the opposite wall were about fifteen kids and their mothers. They were looking nervous, and jittering around on their seats, and punching each other. Most of them had guitars, besides their mothers. Man, there's one time when I'm glad I don't have a mother, and that's at an audition. The mothers never leave the kids alone. They're always straightening their jackets and brushing their hair and telling them remember to do this, Harry, remember to do that. I couldn't stand that. If I was Harry I'd end up slugging my own mother. Mr. Smythe-Jones was always telling me to breathe with my diaphragm and keep the pitch up, but at least he wasn't pulling down my jacket and brushing my hair back every five minutes.

Mr. Smythe-Jones and I sat down on the line of chairs and looked nervous like everybody else. A couple of men and a woman came in and lounged around in an official-looking way. Mr. Woodward leaned on one of the grand pianos, making his gold cigarette lighter appear and disappear, and explained to us what it was all about.

United Broadcasting Company was planning a huge one-hour television show on popular culture. You know, fads.

"There'll be a bit on surfing movies, and one on monster comics, and so forth," Mr.

Woodward said. "Cool it over there, you two guys. They want to have some rock and roll, naturally, and they thought it would be cute to put together a group made up of kids your age. Cool it, you two guys in the green sweater and the red hair. With you cute monkeys I don't know, but it's their beeswax." Everyone giggled nervously.

"This would all be very groovy, except that they picked me to work with you monkeys. Cool it, with the red hair. We're having three auditions, and we're going to pick out six kids. Two will be understudies, but I guarantee that they'll be used, because—cool it, Red—because one kid is bound to get the measles and another will break his leg. Somebody slam that red-headed kid. Okay. When I call your name come on up by this mike and give me something with a big beat. Don't get nervous, just belt it out. Everybody here loves you."

So they began. Some kids played the piano when they sang, but most of them accompanied themselves on guitars. It was the usual bunch: some were pretty good, some stunk; some looked very confident, and some looked scared to death. I sat there and watched them all.

At a thing like this there's usually one kid who's really outstanding. In this case it turned out to be the redheaded kid, which explained why he'd been acting up: he didn't have a worry in the world, and he knew it. He walked up there as confident as could be and belted out a couple of songs with a lot of style and no mistakes. When he finished, he just grinned at Mr. Woodward as if to say: Don't bother telling me how good I am, I already know.

There were two or three others who were pretty good, too: not as good as the redhead, but pretty good. Even so, I had a good chance, and I knew it. Some of them sang a little better than I did, and some of them played the guitar better, but I averaged out better. I had a chance. Except for my problem. Except for being a natural-born loser.

I sat there with the guitar in my lap, my hands clenched tight around the neck so they wouldn't shake. My stomach was full of ice water, and I felt like I needed to go to the bathroom. Oh man, did I envy that redhead. About every two minutes I took a look down into the guitar at the teddy bear. I prayed nobody would notice what I was doing. Not that it was illegal to have a teddy bear in your guitar: it was just so embarrassing.

It's the waiting that kills you. They were going by alphabetical order. My name beginning with an S, I was down at the bottom of the list. The worst part was that I didn't know exactly when my turn would come. I didn't know how many Ls and Ms and Ps there were ahead of me, so that each time one kid finished I had to sit there and shake and quiver until Mr. Woodward announced who was going to be electrocuted next.

So I sat there waiting for death and destruction, and finally Mr. Woodward called my

name. I swallowed, stood, and walked across to
the mike, trying to look casual and relaxed
instead of stiff as a board. I turned around to
face Woodward and the other kids, and struck
a warm-up chord. Then I almost fainted.

Instead of getting a nice full, rich, chord, I
had gotten a muffled clunking sound, as if the
guitar were in the next room. A couple of the
kids giggled.

"What's the matter with the guitar,
cookie?" Mr. Woodward said.

I knew exactly what was wrong with the
guitar. It had a teddy bear stuffed down inside
of it. Anytime you stuff something down inside
a guitar it stops the wood from resonating—at
least partly—and of course the sound goes dead.

My face burned and I started to sweat. "I've
got a mute in the guitar," I said. My voice was
choked and sweaty as my face.

"Well, take it out so we can hear you,
cookie."

At first I thought I would keel over dead; all

I could do was blink and stare at him. Finally I sort of whispered, "I can't."

There was some more giggling. "Why not?"

"I-I have to take the strings off." I reached down through the strings to give him the idea of what was involved, and my hand fell on a handful of teddy bear fuzz. Touching the bear brought back a little of my courage, and the fire on my face started to die out. "It's my special sound," I said. "It's my trademark."

Mr. Woodward laughed. "Okay, cookie, go ahead."

Pretending I was adjusting something, I reached in to touch the teddy again for another shot of courage. I had decided to do one of the Beatles' songs—one I'd worked over with Wiggsy a good deal. I stroked the opening chords, and then I started to sing.

My voice was a little weak and rusty to begin, from the scare I'd had. I looked down into the guitar. At the angle I was holding it I could just make out one of his glass eyes and a bit of the threads of his worn-out mouth; and I swear I saw him wink and heard him say, "Don't worry George, you can do it." And just like that, I knew I could. My voice got stronger and I felt my courage, and I began to look around the room at the audience and belt it out in fine style. Whenever I felt myself growing weak or scared again, I'd just look down into the guitar; and the teddy would stare back at me with a solemn look that told me I had nothing to worry about. I can't explain it; I know that a teddy bear can't talk, but I heard him. I swear it.

So I ran on through the tune, and by the time I got to the end I was feeling so good I added on a little tag Wiggsy had taught me. I struck the last chord and saw all those kids sitting there staring at me silently; and I knew I'd made it. And it was then that my knees went weak and my legs began to tremble and my hands began to shake and my brain closed down for the rest of the day.

"You the kid who says he can read music pretty well?"

I nodded. My throat was too clogged to speak.

"Groovy," he said. "Stick around."

I tried to say something polite, but my throat was still shut up; and besides, my brain had quit on me and I couldn't think of any words. I just nodded my head and walked over and sat down. Mr. Smythe-Jones patted my shoulder. "Top hole, old man," he whispered. "Absolutely top hole."

So we waited around for the rest of the kids to have their turns and then Mr. Woodward took Mr. Smythe-Jones and me back to his office, me still dizzy and trembling with excitement. I sat down in a huge red-leather armchair by a window. You could see barges going up the East River, and way down below the tiny taxi-cabs and buses moving slowly up the avenues. To calm down, I tried to pretend I was Dave Clark or somebody arranging a big movie deal; but it didn't work, so I gave it up and pretended that I was George Stable all in a stew.

Mr. Woodward leaned back in his chair, put his feet up, and flipped the cigarette lighter around a few times. "Here it is, cookie," he said. "Your voice isn't all that groovy, but it's good enough. You've got the confidence, you get around on the guitar pretty well, and the fact that you read music helps. We're going to see some more people, but I want to use you, maybe as one of the understudies. We'll see about that." He slammed open a desk drawer and pulled out a form. "Have your old man sign that," he said, slamming the drawer closed. "We've got to have his signature before we can use you."

And so we left. Mr. Smythe-Jones was so pleased with it all that he called a taxi to take us back to his studio. "You heard what he said about reading music. Fundamentals, George. Cahn't imagine how lucky you are to have a teacher who insisted on fundamentals."

But my problem wasn't fundamentals; it was the piece of paper I had in my pocket. I

thought about it all the way down on the subway to West Fourth Street, and then on down
through Washington Square to Wiggsy's to
return the guitar. I thought about it some more
as I told Wiggsy all about the audition.
Wiggsy took the guitar and shoved it down
behind the counter, and I thought about it as I
said good-bye and walked on home.

I was still thinking about it when I walked
into my bedroom and saw the wide-open bureau
drawer. And it was then that I remembered
that the teddy was still stuffed down inside the
guitar, and the guitar was behind the counter at
Wiggsy's.

CHAPTER FIVE

OP BELIEVES IN simple food and a lot of it. That's another good thing about having a father for a mother: you get the kind of meals you can eat. You take an ordinary mother, she's read in the women's magazines that she's got to serve varied dishes and balanced meals, and she's always coming around with fried liver or chicken croquettes or some other stuff that's likely to make you throw up. Pop couldn't make chicken croquettes if his life depended on it, and as for fried liver, he doesn't like it any better than I do. With him it's hamburgers, hot dogs, and spaghetti, and then back to hamburgers again. For dessert it's ice cream or jelly roll. For variety, about twice

a year on some special occasion like Christmas, he fries some pork chops. That's it. I don't think there's been a roast in the place for five years. It suits me fine. Besides, about twice a week we eat out at Crespino's or Howard Johnson's, so that if I wanted roast beef or chicken croquettes I could get them. What I usually order is the same stuff we have at home: hamburgers, spaghetti, or hot dogs. Pop's hot dogs are flabby and raw, and Crespino's are burnt and hard. That's variety enough for me.

The night I came home from the audition I was starved. I was excited about my chance of becoming rich and famous, and worried about Wiggsy finding the teddy and generally scared just on principle. Being nervous and full of a million feelings like that has the effect of making me very hungry. Pop had cooked up a huge pot of spaghetti and meatballs. I belted away at it as hard as I could, scattering tomato sauce all over the table and pouring the milk in on top of it to wash the meatballs down. My table manners were terrible, but I didn't care and Pop didn't notice. He was busy talking. He likes to brainwash me during dinner, and he was giving me a long lecture on morals that I wasn't listening to, partly because my ears were half-full of tomato sauce.

You would have thought that eating all that spaghetti would have calmed me down, but it didn't. I tried to read a book, and I tried to listen to the radio for a while; I even tried doing my homework, but I kept getting more and more nervous. Finally I just sort of walked around the apartment, touching things.

Pop bore this about fifteen minutes and then he said, "I can't stand you jittering around like that. I'm going over to Florio's for a beer. Go to bed at ten o'clock, hear?"

Out he went, jingling the change in his pocket, and I slumped down in a chair to think. My first idea was to sneak over to Wiggsy's, find some excuse to borrow the guitar back, and rescue the teddy. I decided not to. At that time on a Friday night MacDougal Street would be full of beatniks and weirdos. There would be a lot of hippies in Wiggsy's. Suppose one of the hippies discovered I had a teddy bear in my guitar. Man, it would be too embarrassing. Besides, to be honest, all those people scared me a little, especially at night.

So I had a long phone conversation about nothing with Stanky. Then I made a cold spaghetti and meatball sandwich, sat around listening to the radio, and jumped into bed at eleven o'clock when I heard Pop come whistling up the stairs.

I went around to Wiggsy's at two o'clock the next day for my regular Saturday lesson. It was raining that kind of cold, sad rain you get in New York in October. Pop made me put on rubbers and a raincoat and all that jazz, which bugged me, but I didn't want to get him asking where I was going so I didn't make a stink. The rain pattered on the sidewalk, and the cars slooshed along the wet streets. I walked down

West Third Street, watching scrunched cigarette packs and stuff float along in the gutters,
trying to decide whether I should just confess
about the teddy to Wiggsy, or what.

I hadn't really decided anything when I
reached his shop. I went up the steps. Through
the wet glass door I could see him all blurred,
sitting on his stool behind the counter fooling
around with a guitar. I opened the door and
walked in.

The teddy was sitting on the glass counter,
propped up against the cash register so he sat
facing Wiggsy. It gave me the creeps to see him
there. It was like suddenly finding yourself in a
strange place. It was like suddenly not knowing
where you are.

Wiggsy lifted his big head up and gave me
a slow look. One single cigarette dangled out of
the bottom of his beard. He went on looking at
me for a minute, and then he let his head go
slowly down. He went on striking slow sad
chords on the guitar. He was wearing an orange-

and-white-striped shirt and a red Egyptian fez. Hanging down his chest on a string around his neck was a real baby's shoe, a little white one that was scuffed and used. Next to that great, fat belly, the teddy looked small and helpless; and I was scared. I said nothing.

Wiggsy looked up at the teddy. "You like this song, teddy bear?" he said in a soft, low voice. "I hope so, because I wrote it for you. I call it 'Teddy Bear's Lament.'"

I got hot and red. I opened my mouth and shut it, and opened it again, and finally I blurted out, "How did you find it?"

Wiggsy struck a long, slow minor chord on the guitar and went on looking at the teddy. "You know this kid, Ted? I didn't know you were acquainted." He shook his head solemnly. "Tsk, tsk. I'm surprised at you, Ted, going around with bad companions. You know what happens to fellas who get mixed up with bad companions? They end up on the gallows." He nodded seriously. "Yes sir, on the gallows."

Slowly he reached toward the teddy with his huge hand. With his thumb and forefinger he encircled the neck of the bear. Then he began to squeeze. The skin on the little head got tight, and its one eye began to pop out of the little depression it was sewed into. "Yes sir, Ted, the gallows," Wiggsy said.

I stood silently in the shop, staring at him, too scared to speak or move. He went on slowly tightening the noose until I was afraid the skin would start to split. Then suddenly he laughed and flung the teddy across the shop to me. "I'm just putting you on, babe," he said. "Don't let me bug you."

I stayed in the middle of the shop. "It's sort of a good luck charm for me." I didn't like Wiggsy anymore, and didn't want to tell him anything about me, but I had to tell him something.

He took a cigarette out of his beard and lit it. "That a fact, babe?"

"I took it up to the audition, and I stuck it

in the guitar to carry it back," I lied.

"Did I say there was anything wrong with it, babe? I was just curious. Do you carry it around with you a lot?"

"No. Mostly I leave it at home in the bureau."

He took a suck on the cigarette. "You must take pretty good care of it, huh, babe?"

It was a funny thing to ask; and I wondered about it. "Yes, I guess so," I said.

Then he changed the subject back to my audition and the television show and Mr. Woodward, and I had to tell him what had happened all over again. He told me, sure, he'd always known I was going to be a big success. He prophesied it. Just the other day he'd told some of the local hippies about me and how good I was getting. And he went on for a while this way, saying things that weren't exactly true, and telling me how he'd go over the songs with me and help me to get them down just right. Oh, he spent so much time telling me how helpful he was going to be that he wasted most of my guitar lesson. I didn't care. I didn't like Wiggsy anymore. I didn't trust him, and I was just as glad to get away from him as soon as I could.

I decided not to tell anyone at school about the television show. I didn't want to be a laughingstock in case the whole thing collapsed. They could decide to use bigger kids or cut the act altogether. Since I was a loser, there was a good chance that the government would ban television on the day before the show went on.

I told Stanky, though.

"What are you going to do about your old man?" he asked.

"Aw, he hates television. He wouldn't watch it if you paid him. He'll never know."

"Suppose some friend of his sees it and calls him up?"

"His friends don't watch television, either. They can't stand being brainwashed by the National Association of Manufacturers. If Pop found out that any of his friends were sneaking television programs he'd have them arrested."

"Well, I don't know," Stanky said.

I didn't, either, but I was willing to take the chance. As long as he didn't find out until it was all over, I wouldn't mind being tortured so much. Of course if he found out, he'd sign me up to be drawn and quartered on Mondays, Wednesdays, and Fridays, and burnt at the stake on the other days, and have my allowance cut off for a hundred years besides. But being a hero at school would take some of the pain out of it.

There was still the problem of getting his signature on the release form. For a while I figured I'd just forget it. It was the simplest and safest thing to do. I could get Stanky or somebody who had good writing to do it. I mean after all, Mr. Woodward didn't know what Pop's signature looked like, and besides, he wasn't likely to be suspicious. Most parents would fall over dead if their kids had a chance to go on television. Why should Mr. Woodward think Pop was any different?

The trouble was that I didn't want to do it. I didn't mind lying to Pop a little when it was the only safe thing, and I only felt a little bit bad about using my lunch money for guitar lessons. Forging his signature was another thing, though. I didn't want to do it. I knew especially that if he ever found out he'd feel sorrowful about it. That would make me feel so bad I'd try to be good, and then where was the fun in life?

I had a better plan. It was risky, but it was a way to get Pop's real signature; and later on if he got sore I could always say that it was his own fault.

In school on Monday I gobbled my lunch as fast as I could and went down to the supply room, eating my cupcake and splashing crumbs all over the place. There was an old guy named Glover in charge. He was supposed to keep the place clean and check out supplies, but it seemed to me he spent most of his time reading the *Daily News*. Either he was a very slow reader, or he read the paper over and over again, for you could go down there just before school let out and he'd still be on page four or five.

He had the paper spread out on the supply counter and was leaning over it, working his way through the story headlined:

WHEREABOUTS OF HERMES SAPPHIRE

BAFFLES POLICE

About a week before some thieves had got into the Natural History Museum and swiped a quarter of a million dollars in rare jewels, including the Hermes Sapphire, which was supposed to be the world's biggest sapphire, or roundest, or something. It was a pretty juicy mystery, and I knew I was going to have a hard time prying Glover away from it.

"Glover," I said. "Miss Hornet wants a trip-permission form."

He didn't look up, but went on reading about the Hermes Sapphire. "Got a slip, sonny?"

"No, she only wants one to check something. She said I didn't need a slip."

He went on reading. "You gotta have a slip, sonny."

"She said she'd give you one. Come on, Glover, I'm missing my lunch hour."

Finally he looked up at me, then back down to the paper. He hated to leave the Hermes Sapphire. That was clear. "I'm on my lunch hour, too, sonny," he said grumpily. "Go get it yourself."

I went through the gate, took a slip, carried it back to my home room, and folded it into my math book. It was just a mimeographed form that said:

(Name of student)   has my permission

to take a trip to _____

on _____   (destination)

   (date)

       (Signature of parent or guardian)

That's all it was; but I hoped it would get me a trip to the studios of the United Broadcasting Company.

After school I took the slip over to Stanky's. Stanky has pretty good handwriting, and I got him to fill in the blanks so that it said:

GEORGE STABLE
_____
(Name of student)   *has my permission*
to take a trip to   WHITNEY MUSEUM
_____
on OCT. 30   (destination)
   (date)   _____
                       (Signature of parent or guardian)

I stood by Stanky's desk while he filled in the blanks, trying to imitate Miss Hornet's handwriting as much as possible. "Boy, am I going to get into trouble if they find out about this," he said.

"Sorry about that," I said.

He rabbit-punched me in the arm. "Sorryaboutthatyoucan'thitmeI'mwearingglasses," he said.

"I won't if you get me a piece of your old man's carbon paper."

So he got the carbon paper. I put it in my math book along with the mimeographed form. After that we had nothing to do so we lay around Stanky's room listening to the radio and messing up his bed with some liverwurst we found in the icebox. The Stankys have a maid, but she lets us swipe.

To make my plan work I had to catch Pop sometime when his brain wasn't working too well. The best time for that was some morning when he was being a lousy mother, lying about in bed groaning instead of getting up, and telling me to clean my fingernails.

I had a streak of bad luck, though. The next three mornings in a row he whipped out of bed first thing and began flailing around the place, shouting out orders and making delicious breakfasts of burnt toast and greasy fried eggs. He says, "George, I've got to make sure you get your vitamins," but the truth is that he likes to eat a big breakfast himself. Besides, he always makes a huge mess in the kitchen, and that gives him an excuse to fool around washing the dishes and so forth instead of getting to work on Garbage Man.

I got all into a sweat that I might be too late

turning the permission form in to Mr.
Woodward; or, worse, that he'd wonder what
had happened and call up. Finally, Thursday
night, Pop went over to Florio's to have a beer.
He stayed out late, and when morning came he
just shouted out from his bed for me to get up
and fix myself a bowl of Cocoa Puffs. So I got
dressed and ate, moving as quietly as possible so
that he wouldn't start waking up and clearing
his brain. When I was all ready I went into my
bedroom and killed a little time until I was a
couple of minutes late. Then I took out of my
bureau drawer from underneath my shirts,
where I'd hidden it, the special setup I'd pre-
pared.

The setup was a few pieces of paper clipped
together. On top was the trip-permission form
I'd gotten from Glover. Just under that there
were two or three sheets of old math homework, which I'd put there just in case he started
to thumb through the stack. Next came the
carbon paper, which I'd trimmed down a little

so it wouldn't stick out around the edges. Then came the form Mr. Woodward had given me. Finally, on the bottom, were two or three more sheets of old homework, for disguise. It had taken a little doing to work the thing up, for the signature line on the trip permission slip wasn't in the same place as the line on the television form. But putting a fold in the television form and twisting it off center a little, I had got them lined up pretty well. I knew it didn't have to be exact; nobody follows those signature lines perfectly anyway.

The stack was clipped together tightly, but I was scared that if Pop started fumbling through the pages the whole thing might come apart. Then I might as well just jump out of the window to save him the trouble of heaving me out.

I waited until I was about three minutes late. I got my coat on, grabbed my books and a ballpoint pen, and went out into the living room. Pop was lying on his back, staring at the ceiling. His eyes were open, but the rest of his face looked like it was still asleep. The blankets were all messed up, and his clothes were draped over a chair, not put away in the closet where they belonged.

"I gotta go. I'm late," I said.

He said something that sounded like "Umph."

"You gotta sign this. I'm late."

He made the same noise. I decided it was more unk than umph. I shoved the papers and the pen at him.

He rolled up on one elbow and started to read the note. "Unph," he said.

"Hurry," I said. "I'm late." I was beginning to get shaky.

"Hold your horses," he said. He was beginning to wake up. He read through the note, and then he flipped it up and looked at the piece of homework underneath.

I almost fainted from the agony. "I'm late, Pop," I said.

"Just hold your horses. How many am I supposed to sign?" He flipped up the next piece of paper.

"Just the top."

"Relax," he said, but he flipped the pages down again and signed on the line. "Be home for supper," he said, handing me the stack of papers and flopping down again.

I grabbed the stuff from his hands and peeled out of there. I didn't slow down until I reached Tenth Street for fear that he'd suddenly leap out of bed and come charging up Sixth Avenue after me in his pajamas. But finally I stopped and peeked at the form. The signature was there all right. It was a little smudged, but unless you took a good look at it you wouldn't notice that it was done with carbon paper. I counted on nobody taking a good look. So I threw away the school slip and the old homework, put the television form in my back pocket, and raced all the way to school, because by this time I really was late.

I took the form up to Woodward and Hayes

the next day. The secretary took it into Mr. Woodward while I stood around in all that carpeting and new furniture, thinking that when I got rich and famous I would have an office like it. Famous singers have offices where they sit around with their feet up making deals for records and television shows and getting waited on by a lot of managers and press agents and pretty girls and so forth. My office would have a small private soda fountain in one corner so I could have an egg cream anytime I wanted one. I sat there daydreaming about being rich and famous, and my future office; and I was just getting around to the part where they were giving me my own television show called the *George Stable Hour*, when the secretary came back and said, "Mr. Hayes is busy, but he says to tell you we start rehearsing next Monday. He wants you to come on up right after school."

I told her I'd be up at three-thirty, and left feeling sorry that I hadn't got to see Mr. Woodward flip his cigarette lighter around. I couldn't say I was too disappointed, though. The idea that I, me, George Stable was going to start rehearsing was so exciting that I skipped all the way up to Fifty-third Street to the subway, which was pretty silly for a big kid like me.

On Monday I got the guitar, loosened the strings, and stuffed the teddy inside. Wiggsy was nice about letting me take the guitar. In fact it surprised me how nice he was. I had figured that he'd give me an argument or want some money for a deposit in case I broke something on it, but he didn't. He said, "Take it, babe. Keep it until after the show. Save you running over here for it all the time." As I say, I was surprised.

I made a deal with Stanky to keep it in his closet on the shelf behind the box of sweaters. Stanky said I could practice there if I wanted. Nobody was around Stanky's place much during the day except the maid, and she didn't care what we did.

Rehearsals were great. I wasn't especially

nervous, just nervous enough to feel the excitement. Partly that was because I had the teddy where I could take a quick look at him when I needed to, and partly it was because I was saving the nervousness up for the show itself. It's funny how it works: if you know you're going to get a chance to be really nervous later on, you don't get so nervous beforehand.

There were six of us altogether. Four of us were supposed to dress up like the Beatles or something and sing a couple of songs. The other two would be understudies, in case somebody got sick. They wouldn't decide who would be the understudies until later, Mr. Woodward told us, when they had a chance to find out more about us.

Mr. Woodward was cool. He told us to call him Woody, and, man, did he have clothes. He had about a hundred sports jackets, with a special tie and a special pair of loafers to match each one. The only thing that stayed the same about him was his little mustache and his fake suntan.

But Mr. Woodward was around to watch us rehearse only part of the time. Our real boss was a man named Damon Damon, which I figured to be a fake name. He was musical director for the show. To go with the fake name, he had a fake suntan like Mr. Woodward; and about half the time he talked like a girl. He wore crazy suits with four buttons on the jacket and buttons on the cuffs and buttons on the cuffs of his trousers, too. He always wore some crazy kind of a vest—pink or green or orange—with fancy glass or metal buttons all over it. He called us "dear" and "sweetheart" all the time. Pretty nearly every day he would start off by unbuttoning his jacket to show us his vest. "How do you like my waistcoat this afternoon, sweeties?" he would say. Then he'd tell us where he got it, and how much it cost, or about how some big celebrity gave it to him. The kids called him Damon Damon, the Button King, but we liked him, because he really knew what he was doing. Maybe he acted silly, but he knew all there was to know about music. The kids realized that Damon Damon, the Button King, could teach them a heck of a lot, and they respected him. He was always telling us stories about funny things that had happened to him, or about some famous singers who couldn't read music. I learned more from him in two weeks than I had from Wiggsy and Mr. Smythe-Jones in a year.

Our part in the program was to sing two or three songs somebody had written for us, and to tell a few jokes with the master of ceremonies. The master of ceremonies was going to be Jerry Wastebasket, a famous old comedian everybody had forgotten about who could be hired cheaply. Or at least that's what Damon Damon, the Button King, said.

The jokes they had for us were terrible. For example, Jerry Wastebasket was supposed to ask us if Elvis Presley was our favorite singer, and we'd say, "That old man?" That was supposed to be uproarious. For another example, Jerry Wastebasket was supposed to ask, "Who was that lady I seen you out with last night," and we would answer, "That was no lady; that was my mother." They were terrible jokes all right, but Damon Damon, the Button King, said that it didn't matter, they'd change everything at the last minute anyway.

I figured he was probably right. They were always changing something. First they dressed us up with Beatle wigs and fancy suits. Then they switched us over to crew cuts like the Beach Boys and gave us a surfing song to sing. Then they cut out the surfing song and went back to long hair, more like Freddy and the Dreamers.

It went on and on this way. We'd just get something memorized and they'd change it. Their day wasn't complete unless they changed something. They just couldn't rest comfortably until they'd switched a couple of things around. Damon Damon, the Button King, told us that television was always like that. They'd go on changing things right up to performance time.

If the changes had improved anything nobody would have minded, but they didn't. If they cut out a joke, they put in another one just as bad. At first, when Damon Damon would come in and say, "We're going to make a little change here," we'd all groan. Then we got to wising around, and started cheering when he brought in a change. Finally we got so used to the idea of changes that we didn't say anything, but just set about learning the new stuff.

We went along this way for a week or so, skipping a few days here and there. I was doing pretty well. Between getting used to everything, and being able to look down and see the teddy hidden away in the guitar, I was able to stay pretty calm and cool. I figured I had a real chance to get on the show. The redheaded kid—whose name was Hennings and was naturally known as Little Red Hen—was certain to be the star. A couple of the others had had some experience and were fairly sure to go on. Of the rest of us, one was pretty much out of it. He kept fouling up—missing his cues to come in and so forth. That left it pretty much between me and one other guy, and I figured I could beat him. His voice was a little better, but I read music better and what with the changes they kept throwing at us, that was an advantage; I was usually able to get the new material down the second time through, where it might take some of the others twice as long.

The best part of it all, though, was after the rehearsal, when we'd all go down to the drug-store in the bottom of the building for a Coke. We'd lounge around in a booth, acting like big shots and talking like old experienced television performers. We'd make snotty wisecracks about celebrities, and we'd throw in all the show-business slang we could think of. Man, it felt great being an insider and knowing what it was all about, and I would have sat around the drug-store for hours if I could have. But of course at five o'clock we had to put off being stars and go home and become kids again.

One day I walked into rehearsal, and as usual, Damon Damon, the Button King, had a change to announce. "Sweeties, they want you all to use the same kind of guitar. We've got some new ones for you."

He pointed across the studio to the wall where six brand-new guitars were sitting on the table. I looked at them. They were beautiful all right—the new, modern electric guitars, the kind that have long necks and thin, flat, solid bodies.

A cold chill went up my neck and froze the top of my head, and I felt my stomach sink with despair. For of course the solid-body guitars have no hole in the middle, and no hollow space inside. You couldn't hide a nickel in one of those things, or even something as small as an ant. And there was certainly no place to hide a teddy bear.

 O THERE IT was. After everything I had been through, after all my planning and lying and cheating and worrying, it had come to nothing. I started carrying the teddy up to the rehearsal in my gym bag, and flinging it over in a corner where nobody would notice. There wasn't any problem about that. Most of the kids came up right from school, and they would be carrying gym bags or briefcases and such. There were always piles of sweaters and books and boxes and bags lying around on the grand pianos and the folding chairs. Nobody paid any attention to my gym bag.

But it wasn't the same. The magic didn't

work when I couldn't see the teddy. I don't mean that I went completely to pieces. I just lost my confidence. As long as I had had him where I could see him I knew I wouldn't make any mistakes, except the normal ones. I had confidence. I just *knew* I never fouled up too badly when the teddy was there.

But now I didn't have him, and I just *knew* I was going to foul up. Of course when you know you're going to make a mistake you always do. So I began making little mistakes here and there. Seeing the magic slip away and the mistakes come on like that made me nervous and worried, and of course being nervous and worried made me make more mistakes. I told myself over and over again that there wasn't anything to be nervous about, that I'd done the songs perfectly a thousand times. I told myself that the teddy wasn't magic, that he was just a lousy bag full of cotton wadding. I'd be telling myself this and playing along and suddenly I'd realize that I wasn't paying any attention to what I was doing. I'd break out in a hot sweat and of course about two measures later I'd hit a wrong chord, or play when I was supposed to be resting. Damon Damon would stop us and say, "What's the matter, Georgie? You never made that mistake before."

As I say, I didn't collapse, I just began fouling up here and there, and three days later, when they picked the four stars, I was an understudy. I ought to have guessed from the start: I'm a loser.

Of course there was an advantage to that: since I wasn't going to be shown on television, there wasn't any chance I'd get in trouble with Pop. I'd go up there, watch the show from the side, go home, and it would all be over. I'd learned a lot and gotten some good experience; that was to the good.

Still and all, when I went home the night they picked the losers, I felt lousy. I'd rather have gotten in trouble with Pop. I'd rather have been a winner, even if it meant being drowned four or five times, and boiled in oil on the weekends. As I walked up the stairs I tried to think of some way I could blame it all on Pop, so I would have somebody to be mad at.

Pop wasn't home. I took the teddy out of the gym bag, threw him up in the air, and slammed him with my fist, like a handball.

He sailed across the living room and bounced off Pop's taboret, scattering brushes and tubes of paint all over the place. That made me feel a little better. I started across the room to pick the stuff up. Suddenly I realized that my knuckles, where I'd slugged the teddy, were bruised and sore. At first I thought I'd maybe hit his last glass eye and knocked it off, which would have served him right, but then I realized that his eyes weren't big enough to hurt.

Leaving the paint tubes on the floor where I could step on one and squish it if I had any luck, I picked up the teddy and felt him all over. Sure enough, when I gave him a good squeeze I could feel something hard way down inside. It felt sort of round, about the size of a golf ball or a little bigger.

I was mystified. I couldn't believe that the teddy had had some kind of hard center all along. I was sure I'd have felt it before. Still, how could anything that big get down inside? If it had been something sharp, like a needle or even a fishing hook, you could understand. A thing like that might have worked itself in by accident. But it wasn't anything sharp; it was something solid and round.

I took the teddy over to Pop's drawing table and looked him over closely under his fluorescent light. The bear's cloth skin was made in two pieces, each one half of its body. There was a seam running completely around him: up his back, over the top of his head, down his front, and around underneath to his back again. I turned the teddy around, looking over the seam carefully.

Sure enough, part of the thread in the seam was different from the rest. From the top of the head down the front and partway up the back it was the same brown color as the bear, and pretty dirty from all the junk that had got spilled on him over the years. But from about a quarter of the way up the back to the head, the thread was different. It was brown all right, but it wasn't quite the same color as the other thread, and it wasn't dirty.

Somebody had cut the teddy open and hidden something inside. Man, it bothered me. Who could have done such a thing? Could Pop have done it? Could somebody have found it in my gym bag at rehearsal and sewed something in it for a joke? Of course, it might have been done weeks, or even months before. I didn't think it went back more than a few months, for the new thread was too clean; but still, that was a long time.

I got one of Pop's old razor blades out of the bathroom and took it and the teddy into my bedroom. I didn't want Pop bursting in on me before I found out what the thing was. Carefully I cut down the seam with the razor blade. Slicing the bear made me wince: it was a little too much like operating on somebody.

When I had a hole big enough, I pulled out some of the cotton wadding. Then I looked in. There was something in there all right. I worked my fingers in around the thing, being careful not to mess up everything inside and ruin the teddy. When I had a good grip on it I slowly pulled it out.

It was a soft little chamois-skin bag with a drawstring. I opened the bag and dumped the contents out onto my hand. One look and I knew exactly what they were.

They were smaller than I would have thought. The newspapers had said three-hundred carats or whatever, which sounds pretty big. Actually, the Hermes Sapphire wasn't much larger than a good-sized pea, and the other stones were smaller. There were six of them. From what I remembered from the newspaper stories, two were rubies, two emeralds, and two were sapphires. The Hermes Sapphire was the valuable one, though. The rest were just sort of throw-ins.

Of course there was only one person who could have put them in the bear. Wiggsy. Or some pal of his. I didn't know whether Wiggsy had been in on the actual robbery, or was just taking care of the jewels until they could be sold. It didn't much matter as far as I was concerned, nor probably as far as the police were concerned, either. If Wiggsy was caught with the jewels he'd go to jail for a good long time. It wasn't the kind of thing that Wiggsy would like.

I sat there holding a quarter of a million dollars' worth of jewels in the palm of my hand, getting scareder and scareder by the minute. I didn't know what to do. I went on staring at the jewels, and then I closed my hand so I wouldn't have to look at them.

It wasn't too hard to figure out how it had happened. That first time after the audition, when I brought the guitar back, Wiggsy probably gave it a couple of strokes as he was putting it away. Of course he'd have known right away something was wrong. It wouldn't have taken him long to find the teddy. He'd probably been worried about having the jewels around the shop. If it had been me, I'd have worried. If one of his partners squealed or the cops got onto him some other way, the first thing they'd do would be to search that shop. If they found the jewels, Wiggsy would go to jail for sure. Then there was the chance that somebody might find them accidentally. There were always a lot of screwballs hanging around the place. Wiggsy let them use the guitars and mess around with the music. There couldn't have been very many safe places to hide jewels in that shop.

So he sewed them in the teddy. Or his girl-friend or one of his partners did. But it explained why he was so willing to let me keep the guitar. He didn't want me walking in and out of that shop every day with that teddy bear full of jewels.

How was he planning to get the jewels

back? I didn't know, but it wouldn't have been hard to do. He could easily think up some excuse to ask me to bring the teddy around to the shop. Or he could break into the apartment and get it. Anyone who could break into the museum and steal a quarter of a million dollars' worth of jewels wouldn't have much trouble breaking into our little apartment and stealing an old, beat-up teddy bear.

There was only one way the plan could go wrong. That was if some dumb kid slugged the bear with his fist, and found the jewels. Man, I wished I'd never done it. I wished I'd heaved that teddy down the airshaft ten years earlier.

I opened my hand and stared at the jewels again. Pop was likely to be coming home any time. I had to decide what I was going to do. It was plain that anything I did was wrong. I could tell Pop; but I was scared to death of what Wiggsy would do if he found out I squealed. Besides, if I told, I'd have to tell Pop everything: about the guitar lessons, and the television show, and tricking him into signing the slip, and a whole lot more. Or I could tell the cops: but *they'd* tell Pop, and I'd be back in the same place. I could hide the jewels someplace, and wait until they caught Wiggsy before I turned them over to the cops. But what if Wiggsy wanted them in the meantime? I hated to think about that. He would murder me. I didn't have any doubt of it. He was tough and cool, and if he was gutsy enough to steal a quarter of a million dollars' worth of jewelry, he was gutsy enough to kill a stupid kid who hadn't enough brains not to slug teddy bears. I wouldn't be much trouble for Wiggsy to murder. Big and strong as he was, he could squeeze me to death with his bare hands.

I decided right then and there that I was going to give up the guitar lessons as soon as I got out of this mess. Wiggsy could keep the money, which was up to nineteen dollars now, if I could only get out of trouble. I couldn't quit until he took the jewels out of the teddy, though. He'd have to come after me. He'd come prowling around at night or grab me off the street or—I don't know what.

There was only one thing to do and I did it. I put the jewels back inside the teddy, and sewed him up as best I could, with the stuff from Pop's little sewing kit. I kicked myself for cutting Wiggsy's thread up. If I'd have known, I could have carefully pulled it out, and used it to sew up the teddy again. It was too late for that. I found some thread that was about the same brownish color as the stuff Wiggsy had used. It wasn't exactly right, but if Wiggsy didn't look closely, he wouldn't notice.

That night after supper I took him up to Stanky's. I'd left the guitar there as usual when I'd come home from rehearsal. We holed up in Stanky's room with another bag of those theater nuts, and I spilled the whole story—about having a teddy bear habit, the jewels, and everything. I had to tell someone. I had to talk to someone I could trust.

He said he could understand about the teddy, which was nice of him to say, but probably a lie.

"Let me see the jewels," he said.

I didn't want to cut the teddy open and take them out again, because of the problem of the thread, but Stanky had helped me out on so many things it was only right. So we got a razor and cut the bear open again.

"These are the ones all right," Stanky said. "I remember from the papers. Do you think Wiggsy actually stole them?"

"I don't know. Maybe he's just keeping them for somebody. Let's put them back, I'm getting nervous."

Stanky found some thread about the right color, and he sewed the teddy up, because he could do a neater job than I could.

"What are you going to do, George?"

"I'm going to put him back in the guitar and take the guitar back to Wiggsy. I'll pretend I left the teddy in there by mistake again. What

I'm hoping is that he'll decide that I'm sloppy and careless about leaving the teddy lying around. It might make him think that the teddy isn't a safe place for the jewels. Then when the jewels are gone I'll just forget the whole thing."

"You ought to tell the police."

"Oh no, not on your tintype. If Wiggsy found out I squealed on him, he'd kill me. In fact, he probably would kill me if he even found out that I knew about the jewels." Stanky nodded. "I guess he would."

"Besides, if I told the police Pop would find out everything and I'd be in trouble with him."

We got the guitar down from Stanky's closet shelf, and put the teddy inside.

"You want to come with me, Stanky? I'm sort of scared to go alone."

"Sure," he said. He put on his jacket, and we started out; but just then his mother came in from someplace, wearing a fur coat and smelling like heck from perfume, and she told Stanky he couldn't go.

"You've had a cold all week, Everett," she said. "Besides, your father and I are going to the theater shortly and we want you here when we leave."

I couldn't say that I liked her very much. "See you, Stank," I said, and took off, carrying a guitar containing a quarter of a million dollars' worth of jewels.

There was no moon, and in the spaces between the streetlights it was dark. I cut down across Washington Square Park. About halfway across I wished I hadn't. The beatniks and the bums and the weirdos were out in full force, gathered in little circles around the benches or walking along the paths. They're all night people. You don't see them around the streets much during the day. About five o'clock they come out of their holes, or wherever they hide during the day, and begin to gather in the park or in the bars and coffeehouses along MacDougal Street. They stand around jiving each other and looking bad.

By nine o'clock they're out in a mob. They always give me the feeling that they're looking for something: a fight, or dope, or whiskey, or I don't know what.

So there they were, as I went through the park, with their beards and their funny clothes. As I came along they stared at me. I guess they thought it was queer to see an ordinary kid carrying a guitar through the park at nine o'clock at night. They looked at me, and talked about me, and sometimes one of them would call out, "Hey, kid," and make a wise remark. I had the feeling they all had X-ray eyes and could see those jewels through the guitar. Or that the Hermes Sapphire was so bright it shined through everything. I wished the guitar and the teddy and the quarter of a million dollars worth of jewels would vanish, just disappear. And me along with them, too.

Finally I got out of the park and onto MacDougal Street. The sidewalks were crowded with people. Three or four motorcycle cowboys sat on their bikes along the curb. A bunch of men and women in black leather jackets and crash helmets were clustered around them. Every so often one of the cowboys would gun his engine, making a huge roar. As I went by the motorcycle cowboys stared at me. They didn't say anything, just stared; and I had the feeling that they too knew that I had the Hermes Sapphire in my guitar case.

I turned onto West Fourth Street. People flowed in and out of bars and coffee shops. A mounted cop came slowly up the street. Strange people came and went. They all stared at me. I kept on walking. I didn't look at anyone. Everybody looked so big. Maybe it was the night lights.

Finally I got to Wiggsy's. There was a crowd of people clustered around his stoop, the folk singers and hippies who usually hang around Wiggsy's. They were singing "John Henry," a famous folk song. They all looked dirty and mean, and they gave me the feeling that they'd just come back from doing some evil thing, like torturing people or eating live rats. They were sitting all over the steps, blocking the way. I didn't like the idea of walking up those steps through them; but more than that I wanted to get rid of those jewels.

I said, "Excuse me," as politely as I could, and started up the steps. Most of the people slid over a little to let me get by. Sitting on the top step was a big motorcycle guy in a leather jacket with a zigzag of lightning painted on the front. He didn't move out of my way.

"Excuse me, please," I said.

He just stared at me and didn't move.

"I have to go in there," I said.

He didn't move. "Where you goin' with that geetar, man?" he said.

"I have to take it in there."

He still didn't move. I didn't know whether he was really mean or just trying to give me a bad time or what. "What's a little kid like you doing out this late at night?"

"I have to bring this guitar back."

None of the other folk singers paid any attention. "You blow that geetar, kid?"

"A little bit," I said.

He put his hand over mine on the handle of the case. "Lemme see it, man. I'll show you how to blow that thing."

"Please. I have to give it to Wiggsy."

"I ain't goin' to hurt it, man. I'm just gonna show you how to blow it." His big hand was still over mine; and now he began to unpeel my fingers from the handle.

Then the glass door to the shop opened and Wiggsy stood there, wearing a Chinese-coolie hat and a silver and red shirt which swelled over his huge belly like a balloon, filling the whole door.

He spoke in that soft dangerous voice of his. "Let the kid alone, Sharky, or I'll break you in half."

"I was just jiving the kid, Wiggsy," Sharky said. He tried to sound tough, but I could tell he was scared of Wiggsy, which gave us something in common.

"Well, forget it," Wiggsy said. "What're you doing here, babe?"

I held out the guitar. "I'm bringing this back. I don't need it anymore."

He didn't move out of the doorway. It was plain he didn't want me to come into the shop. "What happened? The show fold or something?"

"No. They got us all special guitars. I figured you'd need this back."

He grunted and took a cigarette out of his beard. "Dig." He took the guitar. "Okay babe, you get home and get into bed before your old man gets tough with you."

I went down those steps and up West Third Street to Sixth Avenue pretty quick. I didn't look around much either.

But I had done it, and now all I could do was to wait and see what happened. Of course the next day I had to go to rehearsal without the teddy, but it didn't matter. Now that I was a loser and more or less out of it, I didn't get nervous. There wasn't anything to lose anymore, so there was no point in getting nervous.

Mainly they were rehearsing the four winners, but they put us two losers up in there too, so that we'd know what to do in case one of us had to substitute. I played through my stuff perfectly, hardly without thinking about it. I didn't make a single mistake. But it was over, and I knew. I felt kind of sad, and when we went down to the drugstore to sit around and act like big shots, I felt like an outsider. It wasn't my scene anymore.

That night I went over to Stanky's to fill him in on what was going on. We went into his room. I told him about being scared going through the park, and Wiggsy looking so tough, and the motorcycle cowboy who tried to take the guitar.

"Sorry about that," Stanky said.

I punched him in the arm. "Sorry about

that," I said, but my heart wasn't in it.

Then we went out to the living room and watched television and slopped some grapes around that we'd swiped and said sorry about that a lot; but as I say, I had no feeling for it. When Pop called at ten o'clock to tell me that if I didn't get my tail home in five minutes he'd warm it for me, I was just as glad; and I peeled.

I cut over Eleventh Street and went down Sixth Avenue to avoid going through Washington Square Park. I was scared of it, and besides, I was afraid I might run into the big guy, Sharky. Sixth Avenue isn't scary. It has banks and drugstores and P.S. 41, and it seems safe.

I went quickly down the avenue, turned into West Fourth, just happening to glance toward our building as I rounded the corner. A fat man with a red fez was going through the door.

I stopped dead. Two thoughts went through my head at once. One was that Wiggsy was going upstairs to tell Pop something. The other thought was that he was looking for me. I didn't know whether to run toward the door or in the opposite direction.

Finally I crept forward along the sides of the building, and peeked through the glass in the door. There was no body in the hall. I opened the door a crack and listened for foot-steps going up the stairs. There was no sound. It spooked me.

I slipped through the door, tiptoed to the foot of the stairs, and looked up.

Wiggsy came out from around behind the stairs, where they kept the baby carriages and bicycles. In that tiny hall he seemed to loom up over me like a huge black shadow, blocking out the light. I stared up at him, and trembled. He was holding the teddy in one big hand.

My mouth dropped open, but nothing came out. Our eyes met. "You left this in the guitar again, babe," he said calmly. "You're gonna lose it if you're not careful." He held the teddy out, and I took it.

"Yes," I whispered.

He patted me on the shoulder. "See ya, babe," he said, pushed past me, and went out the door.

I squeezed the teddy. The jewels were still inside. The only thing I could think was: maybe he knows I know.

I ran all the way up the stairs.

CHAPTER SEVEN

THE SHOW WAS scheduled for nine o'clock Friday night, and by Tuesday everybody was in a panic. We weren't rehearsing at Woodward and Hayes's anymore. We were working in an old movie theater on Seventh Avenue, near Times Square. This was the theater where the show was to be held. All the time we were rehearsing the stage-hands and scenic designers were getting things set up the way they were going to be on Friday night.

Until now all the different acts had been learning their stuff separately. The dancers had been working in a dance studio, the singers in a rehearsal hall, us at Woodward and Hayes, and so forth. Now they brought us all to the theater to put the whole thing together.

It was a mess. In the first place, the big stars had finally come around. That's how it works. All the unimportant people like us and the dancers learn their parts first. The big stars don't join the show until it's almost too late.

Our stars were a singer called Mel O. Tones, a girl dancer named Frisky Legge, and of course the old comedian, Jerry Wastebasket. Naturally the first thing these stars did was to change everything we'd learned. Jerry Wastebasket said that the jokes we were supposed to do stunk, which was right, except that the new ones he got for us were worse. Mel O. Tones said that one of our songs sounded too much like his big number, so Damon Damon had to rush out and get a new one to teach to us. The dancer, Frisky Legge, said that we should stand farther back when she was being introduced; after all, she was the star, and we would distract the audience.

To be frank, I've never seen three more egotistical people. They strutted around the stage, boasting and ordering people around. They all had slaves that followed them around handing them things and getting chairs for them, and saying, "Mahvelous, honey, sheer genius." Every time some little thing went wrong they threw a fit. For example, one time one of Frisky Legge's slaves brought her some Coffee that was too cold or didn't have the right amount of sugar or something. She got red in the face and cursed and screamed and finally flung the coffee halfway across the stage at the director of the show.

Jerry Wastebasket didn't rage around so much. What he did was to boast about himself. He never stopped. He was always going on about what smash he'd been in some movie they made when Washington was president, and how he made a million dollars a month, and how he got mobbed by fans everywhere he went and could hardly get a moment's peace. I didn't notice any mob of fans outside the theater when he came in the afternoon, but he explained that the fans were smart; they knew the cops would chase them away from the the-ater, so they usually waylaid him in the lobby of his hotel. Sometimes it took him almost an hour before he could get his supper, he said.

Actually we six kids weren't doing much rehearsing. The director had to spend most of his time getting the big stars straightened around. Mainly we sat around on the seats in the theater and watched. It was interesting at first, but after a while we got bored listening to Mel O. Tones miss the same notes over and over again. The only good part was that Damon Damon, the Button King, sat behind us making snotty remarks about the stars. He said that it was a known fact that Mel O. Tones was an illiterate and hired people to read his fan mail to him. It was another known fact, he said, that Jerry Wastebasket was always going in and out of mental institutions and had only gotten on

the show be cause he had something on the producer. It was also a known fact that Frisky
Legge was a kleptomaniac. She had been arrested
in Detroit the summer before for stealing a gir-
dle from a five-and-ten, but they hushed it up
when they found out who she was.

Damon Damon would get us all giggling
with his cracks, and then when the director
would turn around and frown at us, he'd give us
a wink and say, "I simply won't tolerate this
giggling, dearies." Then he'd lower his voice
and tell some known fact about the director.

On top of everything else, the show was
about an hour too long. It was supposed to be a
one-hour show, but it had come out to two. So
they were frantically shortening everything,
and of course every time one of the stars got his
part cut down a little he'd get furious and
throw a fit. I'll say this, though: watching the
stars throw fits was a lot more interesting than
watching them sing or dance.

Naturally they expected us all to hang

around late those last few days. On Tuesday I had to call Pop and tell him I was having supper at Stanky's. On Wednesday I called him again to say that Charlie Williams and I had a science project together, and his mother was going to fix us some sandwiches. It was a busy week for lying. I'd already told him that I was sleeping over at Stanky's on Friday night. Of course I was going to sleep there; but in order to get out for the show we'd told Mrs. Stanky that we were going roller skating. So that was another lie.

In any case, we were still hanging around the theater at about eight o'clock Wednesday night when Frankie Sanchez, the other understudy, began to feel lousy. Nobody thought anything of it. All we'd had for supper was stuff you could get out of the candy machines in the lobby: orange drinks and peanuts and chocolate bars. You could get sick on that stuff.

"I got a terrible gut ache," he told Damon Damon.

"There are some benches in the lobby," Damon Damon said. "Go lie down there until you feel better."

So Frankie went out and lay down; and then after a while he came back in, looking gray and sweaty. "I think I better go home, Mr. Damon," he said.

"My, yes. You look terrible, Frankie. Come along, we'll find a cab."

They started up the aisle and out toward the lobby. We watched them go, feeling sorry for Frankie. Frankie wasn't really good enough for the show, and everyone knew it. He'd worked very hard on everything, practicing at home and all that, and he'd gotten to where he could get by if he had to.

They walked up the aisle, Damon Damon going first and sort of leading Frankie out by the hand. Suddenly Frankie jerked loose and tore past Damon Damon, his hand over his mouth. The director turned around. Everyone on stage stopped rehearsing and watched.

Frankie just about made it into the lobby and then he fell down and got sick. We all charged out there. By the time we got to him Damon Damon was in a phone booth and about five minutes later an ambulance came peeling up the street and screeched to a stop right out front. They carted poor old Frankie off on a stretcher, but before they left the ambulance doctor told Damon Damon that Frankie was having an attack of acute appendicitis.

As it turned out, they operated on him right away, and in a couple of days he was feeling good enough to break down and cry about missing out on the show. Afterward we all chipped in and bought him a Sonny and Cher record to make him feel better.

I was the only understudy left. Damon Damon said to me, "George, I absolutely forbid you to get ill. If you feel appendicitis coming on, you must simply grit your teeth and bear it. The minute the show is over you may fall down dead on the stage, but not a second before."

The whole thing started making me nervous all over again. You take five kids about my age, there's always a good chance that one of them will come down with a fever or mumps or break his collarbone or something. It happens all the time. Now there was a chance that I'd get on the show after all. It confused me. Half of me was hoping that one of the other kids would get sick. Nothing serious; nothing you could die from like Frankie's appendicitis. Maybe a rash that looked like measles but went away the day after the show. Or a twisted ankle from basket-ball—not a bad twist, just the kind the doctor says to stay off of for a few days.

On the other hand, half of me wanted them all to stay healthy; for of course there was no way I could get the teddy onto the show. It's one thing to foul up in front of Damon Damon and Mr. Woodward and a few kids. It's another thing to do it in front of forty or fifty million people, including practically everybody in your school. If I got on the show and messed it up, I'd have to commit suicide, or at least run away from home. Really, how could you go back to school if you messed up on a big national television show?

But I knew that if somebody got sick I'd have to go on. There wouldn't be any way out of it; and I began racking my brains to figure out some way to have the teddy around where I could see him, even if it was at a distance. Maybe there was someplace I could stick him down behind some scenery or hanging from a catwalk overhead.

And what was I going to do about the fact that inside of the teddy there were a few little trinkets worth a quarter of a million dollars? Suppose some stagehand happened to kick the teddy out of the way? Suppose somebody tossed it into a rubbish can? Wow. It made me shudder to think of it. When Wiggsy found out that it was missing he'd just naturally think that I'd squealed on him to the police.

One way to do it would be to take the

jewels out of the teddy and hide them in my drawer while the show was on, but it was risky. Anything was risky. For that matter, I wasn't sure that Wiggsy knew I had discovered the jewels. I didn't know anything and everything was scary.

I woke up early Thursday morning and immediately began thinking about where I could hide the teddy if I went on the show. I wasn't up early because I wanted to be, but because Pop was making a lot of noise around the kitchen. When he is having trouble with a comic strip he sleeps late and doesn't say much when he gets up. When everything is going well he leaps out of bed bright and early and starts fixing one of his famous huge breakfasts. He goes singing around the kitchen, slamming pots and pans so that it's impossible for me to sleep. He pretends it's all accidental, but I think he does it because he wants somebody to talk to about his comic strip.

This morning he was making pancakes. I

went into the kitchen. What a mess. He had slopped orange juice around and there were about a hundred bowls all over the kitchen counter. I could tell that he'd started to make the batter in a bowl that was too small, and he'd had to dump it into another bowl. But I couldn't tell what all the rest of the bowls were for, except that he'd got them dirty one way or another.

He was awfully cheerful. "Pancakes, George, pancakes. We're going to have delicious homemade pancakes this morning."

"I figured that out," I said.

"Don't get smart with me, fella, or I'll make you wash the dishes."

"That's okay with me," I said. "It would take me the rest of the day and I'd get out of school."

"Wise guy," he said. He shook the stirring spoon at me, pretending to be angry, and naturally some of the batter splashed on the floor. "Oh well," he said, "you can't make an omelette without breaking eggs."

I sat down at my place at the kitchen table. "You can't make an omelette without spilling a lot of orange juice either, huh, Pop?"

"Okay, wise guy, you can wipe it up."

We keep a sponge right by the sink. We spill a lot around there. I got the sponge and wiped up the orange juice and some of the batter he'd flung around here and there. "I guess Amorpho Man is going pretty good this week."

"I'm working on Garbage Man," he said. "It's really flying. I've got a great new gimmick." He forgot what he was doing and stirred a big plop of batter out onto the counter.

"I never noticed before, Pop," I said. "You cook like you paint. Just heave the stuff all over the place."

"Yes, I know," he said. "It's called action cooking. Now shut up and let me tell you about Garbage Man. See, Rick Martin is no longer going to be a mild-mannered Madison Avenue advertising copywriter. I'm promoting him. He's going to be Rick Martin, mild-mannered

Madison Avenue account executive, in charge of advertising for the far-flung J. P. Astorbilt Enterprises. Fabulously wealthy J. P. Astorbilt takes a liking to the young man, and keeps sending him to various places around the world to investigate troubles in his organization. This way I can get him into a lot of exotic locales. Right now I'm sending him to a certain small Caribbean nation where a junta allied with a certain Iron Curtain power is threatening a takeover which will jeopardize the J. P. Astorbilt sugar mills there. Naturally, Rick Martin will have a trusty Beech twin-engine airplane, as well as his trusty Jaguar. The Beech can turn into a trusty garbage truck with wings. George, it's going to take the comic-book world by storm. What do you think?"

I thought it stunk, but I didn't want to hurt his feelings. "It's great," I said. "And when the bad guys are trying to escape, Garbage Man can bomb them from the air with bags of garbage."

He snapped his fingers. "Right," he said.

"You've got the idea exactly." He started to pour the batter into the frying pan. "Incidentally, speaking of garbage, before you go to school look through your stuff and see if you have any old clothes or toys you don't need. Things you've outgrown. Somebody from the Needy Child's Center came around yesterday collecting stuff for poor kids for Christmas. I told them to come back today."

"All right," I said.

He got the pancakes cooked finally. They were okay, but a little uneven. Half of them were a little too crisp and half were a little too soggy. But that's the way Pop cooks, and I'm used to it. His hamburgers are either raw or hard and black, and his hot dogs are usually limp and rubbery. It's all right, though. You can always disguise the taste of anything Pop cooks with mustard or ketchup or chili sauce or something. So I doused the pancakes with maple syrup and butter, and they tasted pretty good.

Between kidding around with Pop and the

time it took him to cook the pancakes it was pretty late when I finished breakfast. I washed the maple syrup off and was about ready to peel when he shouted out, "Don't forget about the Needy Child's Center."

I didn't have time to mess around. I whipped open my drawer and grabbed a sweater I hadn't worn for a long time, and another one some aunt I didn't like gave to me, and a pair of pants that were too short, and dumped them on the bed. Then I pulled my junk box out from the bottom of my closet—just a cardboard box that said Franco-American Macaroni and Cheese on it. It was full of old toys mixed in with a pretty good supply of dust. I found a windup train, a midget baseball glove, and a couple of other things. I flung these on the bed along with the clothes. Then I grabbed my books and my lunch money.

"I put some stuff out in my room," I shouted. "I gotta peel. See ya."

That afternoon when I went up to rehearsal,

I began looking for a place to hide the teddy, just in case. Whenever I could think of an excuse I wandered around backstage just sort of looking around.

By now the panic was mostly over. The stars had quit throwing fits, and Jerry Wastebasket had cut down on the boasting a good deal. They weren't making quite so many changes, either. Of course they made some changes just out of habit, but they were mainly small things, like switching a word here or there, or having somebody stand a little farther over.

Because there was less confusion, it was hard for me to go places where I shouldn't to look for a hiding place for the teddy. Still, I managed to get around, and after a while I thought of something that might work. Backstage there was what they called the property table. Properties are things people need for the act. For example, there was a fake telephone Jerry Wastebasket needed for one of his comic routines, and there were a cane and a top hat Mel O. Tones carried when he was singing one of his songs, and there was a set of holsters and pistols Frisky Legge used in one of her dance routines. Things like that. There was a strict rule against anybody touching any of the stuff on the prop table, except for the property man. I decided that if I slipped the teddy onto the prop table nobody would think anything of it. Of course, the prop man might think there was something fishy about it, but even he wouldn't want to move it until he found out who put it there, for fear that it might be important. I'd only have to leave it there for five or ten minutes. Then I could stick it under my shirt or something, whip down to the dressing room, and put it away in my gym bag. It was risky; but the point was that by turning my head a little when I was onstage I could get a quick glance at the property table.

So that was settled, and I decided to forget about it. Maybe one of the other kids would get sick and maybe he wouldn't. There wasn't anything I could do about it one way or another. I'd face the whole thing the next night when the show went on.

They let us go early Thursday night. I guess they figured nobody was going to get any better, and they might start getting worse. I got home just about in time for supper. Pop was sitting in his chair, reading the paper. He looked relaxed, and I knew he'd had a good day.

"I guess you finished that sequence on Garbage Man," I said.

"It came out pretty well," he said. "I thought we'd go out to Howard Johnson's and celebrate."

"All right," I said.

"Wash up and put on a clean shirt and we'll go."

I went into the bathroom and washed my hands, and then I went into my room and opened my shirt drawer.

The teddy was gone.

CHAPTER EIGHT

HE TEDDY wasn't in the drawer, and he wasn't on top of the bureau. I couldn't exactly remember where I'd left him. For a minute I just couldn't move. My hands stuck to the drawer handles, and my feet felt as if they were nailed to the door. Then I whirled around and looked at the bed.

The things I had put out for the Needy Child's Center were gone. I began to tremble and shake and my knees got weak. I sat down on the edge of the bed. Then I jumped up and began slamming through the bureau drawers, rummaging through my closet, crawling under my bed, in search of the teddy. I knew in my heart it wasn't any use. Pop had given the bear to the Needy Child's Center. But I kept on hoping that I'd hidden him away someplace and forgotten, or that Pop had accidentally knocked him into a corner when he'd come in for the other toys.

It wasn't any use. It didn't take long to search a room that small. The teddy was gone, and along with him the Hermes Sapphire. I stood in the middle of the room, shaking. Finally I got a grip on myself. I changed into a clean shirt, brushed my hair, and went out into the living room. I undid my belt buckle and began adjusting my belt to give me an excuse for looking down so Pop couldn't see on my face how scared I was. "Say Pop, did you give the Needy Child's Center that old teddy bear of mine?" I said, trying to keep my voice from squeaking.

"I just gave them whatever you put out. Yes, I think there was a teddy bear."

"It was on the bureau," I said. "The stuff for

the Needy Child's Center was on the bed."

"Yes, I guess that's right," he said. "I gave them whatever you had put out."

I had messed around with the belt as long as I could. I buckled it up, and faced him, putting my hands in my pockets for the casual effect. "Well, the thing was, I didn't put the teddy out. He just happened to be there. I didn't want to give him away."

"Oh?" he said. "I'm sorry, I just assumed he was part of the lot."

"No, it was a mistake," I said. My throat was choked up, making my voice gravelly. "I got it when I was a kid. I sort of wanted to keep it."

"I'm sorry. I didn't realize it meant anything to you." He didn't seem very upset, and I thought, you'd be a lot more worried if you knew what was in that bear. "I wonder if there's some way I could get it back?"

"You could go over there after school tomorrow and see about it. They clean and repair all the toys before they distribute them to the poor

children. I imagine they'd give it back to you."
He looked at his watch. "Well, I'm hungry; let's
go."

It wasn't one of the easiest times I ever put
in. Pop was full of good spirits because he had
finished the Garbage Man sequence, and he
went chattering on and asking me questions and
kidding me, and of course I had to kid him back.
As we walked up Sixth Avenue to the Howard
Johnson's he kept pointing out things of inter-
est. "Look at that screwball in the sandals and
the toga," he'd say. Or, "There's old Morris
Fisher. That dirty old man with beard. He used
to be a fine painter in his day."

And I'd have to nod and say, "That sure is
some screwball in the sandals and the toga," or,
"He sure is a dirty old man, isn't he," and so
forth. And all the time my insides were creep-
ing around from place to place. First they'd
climb up one side until they bumped against my
Adam's apple, which was as high as they could
go. Then they'd let go and slide down my spine

and hit on the bottom with a thump; and then they'd do it all over again, just for jollies. To get them to hold still I'd concentrate on my math homework or something. Then, just as I got them all settling back in their places, I would remember that perhaps right at that moment some charity lady was giving the Hermes Sapphire a good washing in naphthalene, or some four-year-old kid was dumping a quarter of a million dollars' worth of marbles into his mouth and chewing on them, and all of my insides would get up and take off for the slides again.

Kidding around with Pop was bad, but eating was terrible. Sitting in the restaurant and jamming down the food I thought I'd go crazy. I kept dropping my fork, and dripping water down my chin, and knocking over the ketchup. I ordered macaroni and cheese, which I figured was a dish which would go down easily.

Right away Pop said, "I thought you didn't like macaroni and cheese."

"They have it at school a lot," I said. "I got used to it."

"Don't have it if you don't want it," he said. "What about the fried scallops? Or a nice piece of pork loin? Waitress—"

"No, no," I said quickly. "I really love macaroni and cheese."

I might just as well have had the loin of pork for all the difference it made. I choked down the macaroni and cheese, and then Pop, since he was feeling rich, insisted that I have a huge banana split, so I choked that down, too. Between being scared and eating all that food my stomach felt as if it had been pumped full of air. All the way back down Sixth Avenue I kept thinking I was about to heave.

But I made it home. "I have to do my homework," I said. I ducked into my room and shut the door and sat there with the math book open in front of me, but I didn't do much homework. Forty-five minutes later I had finished only two problems. I quit. It didn't matter. I had something better to do than go to school the next day, anyway. I got into bed and read until Pop told me to go to sleep. I turned off the light and began tossing and turning. Every time I dozed off I dreamed something terrible: that I was being captured by Nazis with great huge faces; or that monsters were coming from the deep all green and slimey with bloodsuckers hanging off them and their eyes cracked; or that four-legged Mars men who were poisonous to the touch were chasing me. The dreams would wake me up, and I'd lie there in bed too scared to move, until I dozed off into another dream.

Finally a little light came in through the air-shaft window. I got up, dressed quietly, and fixed myself some breakfast.

Pop was asleep on the daybed, but he woke up from the noise I made and came into the kitchen in his pajamas.

"What are you doing up?" he said. "It's only six o'clock."

"I promised Stanky I'd come up to his house

before school," I said. "I have to help him with his science."

"All right," he said. "Make sure you have some fruit juice. Are you sleeping over at Stanky's tonight?"

"Yes," I said.

"I'll be up at *Smash*. I'll get home about three-thirty. You wait for me to get back before you leave." Then he went back to bed.

As soon as I finished my breakfast I sneaked out quietly. Pop was asleep again. It was still half dark in the city. The streetlights were on, but they were pale and cast no light. The traffic was light and the city was quieter than usual. It was cold, and I wished I'd worn a sweater under my jacket.

I began walking up Sixth Avenue. The first thing I needed to find was a telephone booth that had a phone book, so I could look up the address of the Needy Child's Center. It was spooky walking in the city that time of the day. A few workmen in windbreakers were going down the street or standing at bus stops. Every once in a while I would come upon people coming home late from parties. They would be all dressed up and laughing over nothing. With the traffic so quiet I could cross against the light whenever I wanted.

I had trouble finding a phone booth. There was one up near the corner of Sixth Avenue and Eighth Street, but somebody had stolen the phone book out of it. I kept on walking. Finally I came to an all-night lunch wagon. The counter was full, the waitresses were all busy, and nobody paid any attention to me when I went down to the phone in the back. A telephone book hung from the wall below on a chain. I looked up the address of the Needy Child's Center. It was on Ninth Avenue at Forty-fifth Street.

It was warm and cozy in the lunch wagon. The food smells made me feel hungry and sad, and I thought maybe the best thing for me would be to run away for good. I could go out to the Holland Tunnel and try to hitch a ride on a truck. Or I could go up to Grand Central Station, get on a train, and hide in the men's room until the train was out of the station.

But I knew I wouldn't do it. I left the lunch wagon and stood outside, thinking. There was a man standing on the sidewalk in front of me, waiting for the bus. He had his newspaper folded open, and was reading it. I could see a big advertisement:

DON'T MISS TONIGHT.
UNITED BROADCASTING PRESENTS
FADS AND FANCIES,
STARRING JERRY WASTEBASKET,
MEL O. TONES, FRISKY LEGGE,
AND MANY OTHERS

The bus came and the fellow folded the newspaper and got on. It was a good way up to the Needy Child's Center. I could get up there in a few minutes by subway, but the only money I had was my lunch money—forty cents. Besides, the Center wouldn't be open that early. I figured I might as well use the time walking.

It was over thirty blocks uptown and three blocks cross town. In New York crosstown blocks are three or four times longer than up and downtown blocks. I had about three miles to walk. So I started off.

If I hadn't been so worried about finding the teddy the walk would have been exciting. The city was just getting started for the day. As I went along people began unlocking their stores, folding back the iron grilles on delicatessen doors, rolling down the awnings of shoe stores, turning on neon signs in the windows of restaurants. Sometimes I would see a watchmaker putting out displays of watches and jewelry in his windows. Sometimes I would see a Con Edison truck drive up, men get out, and start putting up sawhorses to block traffic. And there was one moment when all the streetlights suddenly went out.

On I went. After a while my feet began to

get hot and sore, and my legs to get tired. I went up Sixth Avenue to Herald Square at Thirty-fourth Street, where Macy's is, and Gimbel's. The department stores weren't open, but there were people in some of the windows putting clothes on the plastic models. The window dressers walked around barefoot so as not to leave footprints. It was funny to see them carrying models around as if they were logs of wood.

From Herald Square I cut up Broadway until I crossed Forty-second Street and got into Times Square. Here there were penny arcades and movie theaters and little pizza places which had been open all night and were still open. There were a lot of sailors around, some of them from foreign ships, wearing strange uniforms. Most of the sailors looked as if they had been out partying all night. They were walking along with girls or standing at lunch counters, drinking coffee and eating hamburgers.

It was getting on toward eight o'clock by

now. The sidewalks were beginning to fill up with people going to work. The traffic in the streets was getting heavy. The sun was beginning to shine down into the streets.

I walked west along Forty-second Street toward the Hudson River. I could see bits and pieces of the buildings on the New Jersey shore across the river. When I got to Ninth Avenue I turned up, and three blocks later I came to the Needy Child's Center.

It was just an old beat-up storefront with Needy Child's Center lettered on the window. The window was painted over halfway up so you couldn't see in. I didn't know what time it opened. It was just about eight. I stood around trying to look through the window, but it was dark inside, and I couldn't see anything. After a while I gave up trying to look in and just stood there, wondering when anyone would come.

At about eight-thirty a woman came and unlocked the door. "Were you looking for somebody?" she asked. She was an older woman, dressed like a teacher, and she seemed nice enough.

"My father accidentally gave away this teddy bear that belonged to my kid brother."

She opened the door. "Let's go inside where it's warmer."

It wasn't all that much warmer inside, though. I took a look around. There were plain board shelves along the walls, all of them jammed up with toys and kids' clothes and blankets and so forth. In the middle of the room there were dozens of huge cardboard cartons filled up with the things they'd collected for the poor kids. There was a fair amount of dust everywhere, a couple of long tables where they sorted things out, and just two bare lightbulbs hanging from the ceiling. It wasn't the coziest place I had ever been in.

"Yes," said the lady, taking off her coat. "Now what was it?"

"My kid brother's teddy bear. When they came to collect yesterday my father gave it away by accident. The baby won't stop crying for it. Pop figured maybe we could get it back."

She nodded. "Surely, of course. If you can find it. We get dozens of teddy bears. You see when these things come in the girls sort them into boxes by kind, before they go out to be cleaned and repaired."

"I see," I said. "Well, would it be all right if I looked?" With all those boxes it was going to take me a year.

"Surely. Now, a teddy bear? You'll find some boxes marked 'Stuffed toys for cleaning.' You might try them."

She sat down at one of the long tables and began working on some papers, Humming "Happy Days Are Here Again" all the while. I went to work on the boxes. She was a good, loud hummer, and I wished she'd stop, or at least try humming something sad and gloomy. "Happy Days Are Here Again" was driving me crazy.

The cardboard cartons were these huge kind

about five feet tall, big enough for a man to get inside. What I had to do was find the ones marked "Stuffed toys," drag them out one at a time to the clear space in the middle of the room, dump them over, and then toss the stuff back in until I came upon the teddy.

Man, was there dust over that place. I hardly got through the first box before I was covered with it—my clothes, my face, my hands. By the time I'd gotten through the second box I was not only dusty, but sick and tired of looking at stuffed dogs, stuffed cats, stuffed Mickey Mouses, and stuffed spacemen, and stuffed Ringo Starrs, and I don't know how many stuffed bears. But no teddy.

I went through seven boxes. It was eleven o'clock before I got finished. I went over to the lady, trying to dust myself off a little.

"I didn't find it," I said.

"Oh dear, that's too bad. Very likely it's already gone out for cleaning." She looked at her watch. "Aren't you going to be late for school?"

It was very polite of her to put it that way. I was already two hours late.

"We have teacher's conferences at my school today," I said. "That's why I had a chance to come out and look for my brother's teddy," I said.

"I see," she said. "Perhaps you know what time it was picked up?"

I thought about that. Pop hadn't said. "I don't know," which was about the first truthful thing I'd said since I'd gotten up that morning.

"If it were picked up before noon there's a good chance it's gone out for cleaning. I don't know what I can do about that."

I was tired and hungry and a little sick from being scared so much of the time. "Maybe I could go over to the cleaning place?"

"I don't think they will let you in."

"Maybe I could ask them."

"You can try, surely. It's the Apex Rug Cleaners, on West Eighty-eighth Street. Here." She scribbled down the address on a piece of scratch paper and gave it to me.

West Eighty-eighth Street was about forty blocks away. I was too tired to walk all the way up there, and besides, time was getting on. I walked over to Eighth Avenue and took the subway up. That left me twenty cents—just enough to get home on. I was starving. In every station the subway stopped at I could see chocolate bars and gumdrops in the candy machine, but if I spent as much as a penny I'd have to walk all the way back down to the Village, about eighty blocks away.

The Apex Rug Cleaners was on the bottom floor of an old beat-up building off Amsterdam Avenue. There was a counter right there when you came in the door, and behind that a lot of machinery giving off steam and people working around vats of stuff, and the sharp smells of chemicals.

The woman behind the counter was fat and ugly. Her hair hung down in straggles and there were a couple of good big warts on her face. I told her the whole lie about my kid brother and so forth as politely as I could.

"That stuff ain't here, kid," she said crossly. "Even if it was I couldn't let you have nothing."

I got sick all over again. "Could you tell me where it went, please?"

"I'm busy, kid. Don't bother me," she said.

"Please, it's important."

She shrugged. "It's in the drying rooms. Around the block. But they won't let you have nothing, either. Now scram."

I scrammed. It was past twelve-thirty. I burst out of the Apex Rug Cleaners and ran back to Amsterdam. What she meant by around the block wasn't exactly clear. I ran up Amsterdam, looking for signs. There were mainly shops and cafeterias and so forth along the avenue; it didn't seem like the right kind of place for a drying room. When I reached Eighty-ninth Street I ran around the corner and stopped. There were no signs out. Most of the buildings looked like private apartment houses, but mixed in here and there were a few that looked as though they might have factories in them. I walked up one side of the block opening all the likely looking doors, trying to find clues or signs. I went up to the end of the block, and then I crossed over and started down the other side. I was pretty nearly down to the end of the street before I found it.

It was nothing more than a little entrance-way with stairs leading up. There were no signs, but I could smell that chemical cleaning smell. I went on up.

At the top there was a big iron fire door. I pushed it open, and walked into a huge, dark loft room with a great high ceiling from which hundreds of rugs dangled almost to the floor. It was an eerie place. The rugs cut out the light, and they muffled all sounds from the street. Here and there were little aisles through the rugs, like paths through a forest. Back in the dark distance I could see workmen moving around. The rugs muffled the sounds of their footfalls, and they moved through the gloom as silently as shadows.

Next to the door an old man with silvery hair and a grandfather look sat at a beat-up wooden desk. The top was sprawled with papers. There was a thermos bottle standing on the papers, and as I came in the old grandfather was unwrapping a sandwich from some waxed paper.

"What do you want, sonny?" he asked.

I told him the lie about my kid brother's teddy bear. "The woman over at the other place said I could come over and get him."

"She did, did she?" he said. "I guess I'll decide about that. Which woman?"

"Some woman behind the counter. She's sort of—sort of big."

"Well you can trot right back around there and tell her she's got nothing to say about what goes on over here."

"I didn't know you were the boss, or I'd have come here first, sir," I said.

"I'm glad somebody realizes," he grumbled.

"Now what was it you were looking for, sonny?"

I told him all over again. While I was talking he opened the thermos bottle, poured some coffee into the cap, and took a big bite of the sandwich. He chewed away at the bite of sandwich. It was cheese and bologna. I could smell the mustard. I got finished telling my lie and waited. He chewed away at the bite of sandwich slowly and carefully, as if he were inspecting it with his teeth. When he'd got it mostly chewed he took a big swallow of coffee and chewed that too, for a while. Finally he put the sandwich down on the sheet of waxed paper and stood up. "Brown, you said it was?"

"Yes sir," I said. "Brown."

He walked off into the jungle of rugs and disappeared. I waited. There was an old-fashioned alarm clock on his desk. It ticked loudly in that quiet place. I waited as the time went from five after one to one-ten and then to one-twenty. Time was adding to my problems. Pop had said he'd be home at three-thirty to get me ready to spend the night at Stanky's, which probably meant he'd be home by four. I had to be home first.

Finally the old grandfather came back through the dark, gloomy aisles of the forest with silent footsteps. He was carrying something in his hands. I held my breath. He came out of the woods, went around behind the desk, and dropped the teddy down next to the sandwich.

"That what you looking for?" he said.

"Oh yes, sir," I shouted. "Oh thank you." I reached out.

He put his hand on the bear. "Not so fast, sonny," he said. "Not so fast there."

He sat down in the chair, picked up the sandwich, and took another bite of it. I waited, jiggling around from one foot to the other, while he chewed the bite over carefully and washed it down with a swallow of coffee from the thermos top.

When he finished he said, "Everything comes in here on an invoice; everything goes out of here on an invoice. You get me an invoice from Mrs. Saddler, I'll give you the bear."

"Please," I begged. He had taken his hand off the teddy in order to drink his coffee. If I grabbed it quickly and ran, I could probably be out the door before the old man could even get around the desk. I licked my lips.

He picked the bear up, kicked open the bottom drawer of the desk, and dropped the bear in. "Sorry sonny, can't do it. I'm the boss here. We do things *my* way."

I felt like crying. "Please?"

"Nope, I can't."

He'd made up his mind and there was no point in arguing. "Who is Mrs. Saddler? Is she the lady at the Needy Child's Center?"

He picked up the sandwich, and I thought I was going to have to go through all of that chewing again, but I guess he decided he'd given me a hard enough time already, for he spoke before he bit. "I never laid eyes on the woman, sonny. I recognize her signature pretty good, though." He gave me a stare to tell me not to try forging an invoice.

"I'll get the invoice," I said. "Will you keep the teddy here until I get back?"

"I'll do that much for you," he said. He bit into the sandwich, and I peeled.

I was still in a mess, but it was a better mess than I had started the day with. If the old grandfather kept his promise, I could get out of it. I ran to the subway, and then going downtown I carefully thought everything out.

Mrs. Saddler was probably the nice lady at the Needy Child's Center, but even if she wasn't, she'd know who Mrs. Saddler was. The trouble was that I'd spent my last twenty cents for the subway trip down to the Village. What I had to do was beat it home and grab some money and something to eat. There was still time before Pop got home. Then I'd call up the Needy Child's Center to find out who Mrs.

Saddler was, and where she was, and would she sign the invoice, and all the rest of it. Then I'd go hide someplace until three o'clock. I'd come home just as if I'd been in school all day, pack my stuff, and go get Stanky. Then we'd pick up the invoice, get the bear, and have plenty of time to make it to the theater by six o'clock. We were supposed to get there early to get into our costumes, and have time to make changes, just in case.

So I had a chance. I got out of the subway at Christopher Street and tore down West Fourth to home. It was just about two o'clock as I hit the living room. I didn't have much time, but I had enough. The first thing I did was to make two huge peanut butter sandwiches and stuff them into my mouth as fast as I could, washing them down with nearly a quart of milk. Then I went into my room to get some money out of my savings bank.

Wiggsy was sitting on my bed, smoking a cigarette and flicking the ashes on the floor. He was holding a gun in one hand, hanging down between his knees. He was holding it as carelessly as if it weren't anything more than a bottle of soda pop. It was the casual way he had with that gun that got me.

"Home a little early from school, ain't you, babe?" he said in that soft voice.

CHAPTER NINE

OW COME YOU home so early from school, babe?" he said softly.

I was so scared my throat closed and I had to whisper. "I played hooky," I said.

"Bad habit, babe." He dropped the cigarette butt onto the floor and slowly crushed it out with his heel. He was wearing a red silk shirt with big patches of blue worked into it, but he had no funny hat on and no cigarettes in his beard. I figured he wanted to be as inconspicuous as possible.

"Okay, now listen, babe," he said. "You just sit down there on the floor with your back against the door; and you fold your arms across your chest; and you don't move a muscle. You got it, babe?"

I nodded and sat down the way he told me.

"Now listen, babe. If anyone comes in you keep cool and quiet. If they knock on this door or try to come in, you don't say nothing—until I give you a signal with my hand, like this. You got that so far, babe?"

I nodded.

"Then you tell 'em you're having a rest; you'll be up in a while."

"Now." He raised the gun up so the black hole in the middle was pointing dead center between my eyes. I stared past the hole down the gun barrel to the black hairs on the knuckles of Wiggsy's big hand.

"Now babe, we're going to have a little game of truth or consequences," he said in his soft voice. "I'm going to ask some questions, and every time you give me a wrong answer I'm going to take my big hand and pound the right one into you." His voice got softer and lower.

"And while I'm pounding you, you're going to sit there quiet as a mouse. Because if you start shouting and screaming I'm going to take this gun and blow the top of your head clean off." His voice dropped to a whisper. "You hear me, babe?"

I couldn't speak, so I nodded my head.

"Okay, question number one: what time does your old man get home?"

I couldn't speak, and had to clear my throat. After all our whispering, the noise seemed loud and scary. "About three, but he isn't regular."

"Not before three?"

"I don't think so, but I can't tell for sure."

"Okay, question number two: who sewed up the bear?"

Wiggsy knew everything. "I did, Wiggsy," I whispered.

"Not your old man."

"No. He doesn't know anything about it."

There was a long silence. He let the pistol drop a little and stared at me. After a while he said slowly, "You know, I don't believe that, babe."

"So help me, Wiggsy, it's the truth."

He raised his hand and started to swing. I jerked back; but he stopped swinging and held his hand in the air about a foot from my face. "Please Wiggsy, it's true. He doesn't know anything about you at all. All I wanted was for you to take the jewels back and forget the whole thing. That's why I left the teddy in the guitar that time. I was hoping you'd take the jewels out." I stared at him, and the sweat streamed down my face. His breath was coming hard and the red and blue shirt rose and fell over his huge belly like a tent in the wind.

"I'm warning you, babe," he said. "I'll clobber the whey out of you. I mean it."

"Please, it's true."

He took out a cigarette, lit it, and threw the match on the floor. For a while he sat there holding the pistol, thinking about it. I couldn't take my eye off that gun, it scared me so.

"You put the bear in there so I'd take the stuff out?"

"Yes."

"Well you want to know something, babe? I been here since ten o'clock this morning turning the place upside down. I didn't find that bear. You want to know what I think? I think it's down at the police headquarters on Centre Street being torn apart by a dozen technical specialists. What do you think about *them* onions, babe?"

"It's not there, Wiggsy," I said. "I know where it is."

"Yeah? Do tell."

So I told him the whole story; about getting up at six that morning; and the Needy Child's Center; and the Apex Rug Cleaning Company; and the old grandfather and all the rest of it. He just sat there staring at me, the gun dangling between his knees, watching my face to see if I was lying. When I finished he went on watching me for a while longer, smoking and squinting his eyes and thinking. Finally he said, "I don't think you could have made that story up, babe." He stood up. "Okay, let's go get it."

He started to shove the gun under his shirt, and I leaned forward to get up; and just at that moment we heard Pop turn the key in the lock to the apartment door. I stopped stock still, frozen. Slowly and silently Wiggsy pulled the gun out of his shirt and swung it around to point straight down at the top of my head.

We heard Pop come into the apartment, shut the door, fling some stuff down someplace, and tramp out to the kitchen. After a minute he began rattling some dishes around. He was fixing tea. I was pretty sure of that. He liked to have a cup of tea and maybe a doughnut or something for a snack when he came home from work.

Wiggsy didn't move. He stood over me, his great stomach above me like a rock about to fall. I stayed still, half standing, half sitting, not daring to move. My legs began to fall asleep, and my back was sore and cramped.

Pop went on messing around with the tea. There was no telling whether he would come into my room or not. I was supposed to make the bed every day and sweep it out once a week and keep my clothes picked up and so forth. Every once in a while he'd stick his head in to see if I was keeping it clean. Then of course he would come in to put the clean laundry in my drawer, or get the dirty stuff. But then sometimes he might just walk in for no reason.

What was most likely was that after a while Stanky would get to wondering where I was and call up. That would get Pop and Stanky to asking a lot of questions of each other, and who knew what that would lead to.

I had just finished thinking this when the phone rang. Pop picked it up and said hello. Small as the apartment was, and quiet as we were being, we could hear every word.

"No, he's not here," he said.

There was a long silence. Finally he said, "Hold it, hold it, what television show? I don't understand. Are you sure you have the right number?"

Another silence. "Yes, yes, Smythe-Jones, that's right, but I think maybe you want one of his other students?"

Then silence again. I could hear Wiggsy's watch ticking. Then I could hear Pop shuffling around for his pipe and his tobacco. The silence went on and on. My legs were asleep, and I knew they were going to hurt when I tried to walk on them again. There was silence and ticking and the sound of blood rushing through my body.

Finally Pop spoke. "Mr. Woodward, you may very well have a release sheet with my name on it, but I guarantee you I know nothing about the whole thing. Are you positive you have the right boy? Yes? Well, it must be right. It must be something Smythe-Jones arranged, but I can't understand why he didn't talk to me about it."

He stopped talking. I started to shift one

leg to ease the cramp in my back. Wiggsy
snapped the muzzle of the gun at me, and I held
still.

"I don't get this whole thing," Pop was saying. I could tell he was getting sore at Mr.
Woodward. "You say some kid broke his arm
riding his bike and George is supposed to take
his place on the show tonight. Frankly . . ."
There was a short pause. "Yes, but frankly I'm
not sure I want George to have anything to do
with it . . . Well, that's your problem, Mr.
Woodward. Heck no, I didn't sign anything. . . .
All right, calm down. Yes, I'll bring the boy up
right away. I'm as anxious as you are to find out
what's going on. He must be on the way home
from school now. In fact, he should be here
now. I'll run out and catch him, and bring him
right up. . . . Well I don't know, Mr.
Woodward. We'll see. Good-bye."

We heard the phone bang down and then
some quick tramping around as Pop got his coat
on, and then the sound of the door slamming,

and Pop's footsteps getting softer and softer as he went down the stairs.

Talking about losing. After all these weeks of auditions and rehearsals and lying and cheating I'd finally got my break; and there was a good chance I'd be dead just about the time the show started.

For a long minute neither of us moved. Then Wiggsy said, "On your feet, babe." He slipped the gun into his shirt. I tried to stand up, but my legs were completely numb, and I started to fall.

"My legs are asleep, Wiggsy."

He grabbed me by the front of my shirt, jerked me up, and spun me around to face the door. "Move, babe. And keep it cool."

I went out of the apartment and down the stairs ahead of Wiggsy, stumbling and wobbling on my numb legs. Wiggsy kept right behind me, half carrying me by the back of my collar. For all that fat, it was amazing how fast he could move when he wanted to.

At the bottom of the stairs he eased forward and looked out. "Which way did your old man go?" he asked.

"I don't know," I said. My legs were beginning to thaw out, and they prickled.

He banged me on the back of my head with his knuckles; not hard, but enough to make my eyes sting. "Up Sixth Avenue, probably."

"Better be right." He shoved me out, and we began going up West Fourth Street as fast as we could and still look natural. We got up a couple of blocks and then a cab came out of Jones Street. Wiggsy flagged it down, and we got in.

"Where's this place at, babe?"

"You mean the laundry?"

"Yeah."

"Eighty-ninth Street off Amsterdam," I said.

He told the driver. We turned onto Sixth Avenue and headed uptown. "Wiggsy, he said he wouldn't give it to me without an invoice from Mrs. Saddler."

"Don't worry, babe," he said. "I'll get it."

He lit a cigarette, and after that we said nothing. I looked out of the window, trying to think of an escape. I really didn't want to make myself think. I just wanted to sit there frozen and still and just do what Wiggsy told me.

Wiggsy wouldn't want to kill me. He was mean and tough and cool, but he wasn't the kind of guy who liked to kill kids. I guess he was probably a little crazy, the way most of the beatniks and weirdos around Greenwich Village are, but he wasn't really crazy. I mean he wasn't a lunatic or anything like that. He ran his store and taught guitar lessons and so forth; a maniac couldn't do things like that.

So he wasn't likely to kill me because he was nutty or because he got a blast out of killing kids. He would kill me only because I knew about the jewels.

The cab driver took us straight up Sixth Avenue, past the candy store where Pop got his newspapers, past the Howard Johnson's, past

P.S. 41, where I'd gone to school up to the sixth grade, past the lunch counter where I'd looked up the Needy Child's Center only that morning. It hardly seemed that it could be the same day, or even the same week. We went straight up Sixth Avenue, and then through Central Park, and came out at Seventy-second Street. From here it took us only a few minutes to get up to Amsterdam and Eighty-ninth Street.

"Let us out at the corner," Wiggsy said. He paid the cabbie, and we got out. Then he put his arm around my shoulders in what seemed like a friendly way and grabbed hold of the muscle on my upper arm.

"Okay, babe, open your mouth at the wrong time, and I'll squeeze the muscle right off your arm," he said. He flung his cigarette away. "Where's the place?"

I pointed. We walked up the street and into the entranceway. Wiggsy sniffed. "It smells like a cleaning shop," he said. "So far you're okay."

We climbed the stairs, opened the door,

and Wiggsy pushed me into the gloom of the rug forest. He stood just behind me, his hand lying loose and casual on my upper arm. Wiggsy squinted around the dark, smelly room at the rugs and the shadowy men working in the aisles. Then he turned to the desk.

The old grandfather with the silvery hair was gone. In his place a young fellow sat with his feet up on the desk, tipped back in his chair reading the *Daily News*. On the page folded back toward us there was a small headline which read:

MUSEUM HEAD TO COPS: SOLVE SAPPHIRE HEIST OR CALL F.B.I.

I jerked my eyes away and looked at the man. The man seemed to have the measles, for he kept scratching himself. He looked around the edge of the paper. "What can I do for you fellows?" He gave his chest a quick scratch.

Wiggsy gave my arm muscle a little warning squeeze. "The boy was here looking for his teddy bear this morning. He says you were keeping it for him."

The scratcher shook his head. "Don't know anything about it."

Wiggsy gave me a look.

"It was a different man, Wiggsy," I said quickly. "An old man with white hair."

"That right?" Wiggsy asked the man.

The scratcher crossed over an arm and went to work on his left side. "Yeah, that's Carl. He was here before. Well, I don't know anything about it. Why don't you come back on Monday morning when Carl's here?" He finished cultivating his side and went to work on his stomach.

Wiggsy let go of my arm and put his hand on my head. "I'll tell you, fella," he said, "the boy is pretty cut up about it. I'd like to do something about it tonight."

"Teddy bears? Listen, we get hundreds of teddy bears."

I said, "He put it in that bottom drawer. He

said he'd keep it for me." I cleared my throat. "I saw him put it in there."

The scratcher quit harrowing himself, bent forward, and opened the drawer. Wiggsy and I leaned over the desk to see.

The drawer was empty. "Maybe he switched it to another drawer," I said.

The scratcher sighed and closed his eyes as if he were exhausted. "Look, kid." Then he opened all the drawers in the desk one by one. There was no teddy bear in any of them.

Wiggsy reached into his hip pocket and took out a roll of bills. He unwrapped a five-dollar bill from the roll and folded it up very small. "The boy is all broken up over it," he said. He laid the folded five-dollar bill on the desk and put the old alarm clock on top of it.

The scratcher went to work on his chin. "It was in the stuff from the Needy Child's Center, right, kid?"

"Yes."

"Yeah, well maybe Carl put it back with

the rest of the stuff. Let me check." He walked off into the jungle, scratching his back, and disappeared in the gloom. In five minutes he came back, carrying in each hand a bear. He held them up for us to see. "This what you were looking for?"

Wiggsy snatched them out of the scratcher's hands and began examining them quickly, but I knew right away neither of them was the right teddy.

"They're not right," I said.

Wiggsy grunted, and dropped them onto the desk.

The scratcher patted me on the shoulder. "Well, teddy bears are all pretty much the same," he said. "You just take one, kid. On the house."

Wiggsy shook his head. "You know how it is, the kid wants his own back."

The scratcher shrugged. "Maybe Carl took it home with him."

Wiggsy nodded, and his eyes narrowed. He

was thinking that maybe Carl had discovered the jewels and taken them home. "What's Carl's phone number?"

"He hasn't got a phone," the scratcher said, slipping his hand under his shirt to get at his belly. "He lives in a rooming house down on Avenue B someplace." He gave Wiggsy a look. "Okay, okay," he said, "maybe it's in his Social Security file."

He walked back into the jungle again. When he returned he was holding a slip of paper, which he handed to Wiggsy.

"Thanks," Wiggsy said. "Okay, babe, let's split."

Now Wiggsy's hand was on my arm, squeezing, and we were hurrying again; hurrying down the street and around the corner; hurrying across Amsterdam, where we caught a cab going downtown. Wiggsy sat still, staring straight ahead, his arms wrapped around his huge belly as if he were holding it from flying off like a helium balloon. During the whole trip nobody said anything. I stared out the window on my side. My arm hurt where Wiggsy had been squeezing it and my stomach was sore from being scared so much. I couldn't think anymore. I looked out the window and watched the scenery go by.

By the time we got down to the address the scratcher had given us it was toward the end of the afternoon. It was getting cool and dark. The kids were quitting their games and going in to watch television or do their homework and eat their suppers. I wished I were doing the same. I wished I were just an unimportant kid who never had anything interesting or exciting happen to him, just an ordinary kid who went to school and played stoopball in the afternoon and did his homework in the evenings. I wished I could erase from the past my ambitions to play the guitar; erase Wiggsy and Mr. Woodward, and Damon Damon and all the rest of them. But you can't erase the past.

The neighborhood around Avenue B, where

Carl lived, was old and sort of slummy. The buildings were dirty, and there was garbage spilling out of the garbage cans lined up along the curb. All up and down the block people were sitting on the front stoops, even though it was getting cold. A few kids were still playing ball or horsing around among the cars parked along the street.

We got out at Carl's address. An old woman wrapped in a beat-up fur coat was sitting on the stoop. "We're looking for a fella named Carl," Wiggsy said.

"Top floor. Five rear," she said. "But he ain't in. He goes out to eat now."

"We'll go up and wait for him," Wiggsy said.

We went in. There were cigarette butts and candy wrappers and junk like that on the floors, and a thick smell of garbage everywhere. Kids had written their initials and some dirty words on the walls with crayons and marking pens. We started up the stairs. Wiggsy shoved me along ahead of him. He was breathing hard and grunting as he heaved that huge fat stomach up the stairs, but he was going fast and I had to rush to keep ahead of him.

The light in the fifth floor was out, and the hall was dark.

Wiggsy lit a match and examined the door to the rear apartment. The number was mostly worn off, but there was enough to read: 5R. The match burned down and went out.

Wiggsy knocked. We waited in silence. From five stories below came the faint sounds of kids shouting and the grinding of a bus pulling away from the curb. Nobody answered. Wiggsy heaved the door with his shoulder. It wobbled, but it didn't give.

He lit another match and bent over to inspect the lock. After a moment the match burnt down to Wiggsy's fingers. He cursed and flung it away. Then he took something out of his pocket, and began poking it in the lock. He was bent over the lock, blocking my view, and I couldn't tell whether he was working with a file or a skeleton key or a wire or something else. He cursed softly to himself as he worked. Every minute or so he glanced back at me to make sure I wasn't going to make a run for it.

There wasn't much chance of that. He was standing only a couple of feet from the head of the stairs. If I tried to lunge past him he could grab me just by reaching out with his big arm.

In the other direction there was a flight of stairs going up to the roof. Because of the dark I couldn't see up there very well, but I knew at the top there would be a metal fire door which opened onto the roof. In two big steps I could be on the stairs. It wouldn't be much of a head start on Wiggsy, but it might be enough. Wiggsy could move pretty fast for a fat man, but on the roof it would be dark, and there would be television aerials, with their guy wires, and low walls and chimneys. I know. I'd been on New York roofs plenty of times. Dodging around all that stuff I could make better time than Wiggsy could. Some places in New York you can cover a whole block—sometimes go around the block—going over the rooftops. Once I got a couple of roofs away from him I could dash down the stairs of another building, or slip down a fire escape or even hide behind a chimney.

There was only one trouble with the whole idea. Those doors are supposed to be unlocked so people can get out in case of fire, but in these old buildings half the time somebody puts a padlock on them to keep out thieves or to keep kids off the roof. Suppose I made a run for it and the fire door was locked? I'd be trapped; and Wiggsy would just laugh and smack me around a couple of times.

I was thinking all of this when Wiggsy said, "Got it," and pushed old grandfather Carl's door open. The apartment was dark. Wiggsy leaned into the hall listening, in case Carl was asleep in there. It was quiet. Somewhere a big alarm clock ticked. We went in. Wiggsy closed the door behind us. Then he turned on the light.

We were in the kitchen. The place was clean and tidy, the way an old man will keep things. There were no dirty dishes around, and the food was all neatly stored behind the glass doors of the cupboards.

The teddy was sitting on the kitchen table, propped up against a ketchup bottle. We stopped dead and stared at it.

It seemed to be sitting there patiently waiting for us. I almost expected it to say something like, "What took you so long?" or "How did you manage to find me?"

Then Wiggsy grabbed it. He squeezed it with both hands, feeling for the jewels. "Good," he said. "You're lucky, babe. You were telling the truth."

I didn't say anything. There wasn't anything for me to say. What was he going to do with me now?

He jammed the teddy bear under his shirt,

lit a cigarette, and sat down in a chair by the kitchen table, thinking.

I stood, waiting. Then I heard from somewhere up above a soft thud, a dull thump. I knew right away what it was, for I'd heard it many times before. It was the sound of an unlocked fire door banging in the wind.

 EVERYTHING WAS silent except the ticking of the alarm clock. Wiggsy went on smoking and thinking. Every once in a while he would turn and stare at me. I knew he was trying to decide whether or not to kill me. First he would look at the cigarette, and then he would look at me, and then back at the cigarette. He was cool. He was taking his time about it.

Finally he said, "Okay, babe, let's go." He motioned for me to go out the door ahead of him. I opened it and went out into the dark hall. Wiggsy turned back to snap the lock behind him. I ran.

In two strides I hit the stairs going up and

charged for the top. It took Wiggsy a couple of seconds to realize what had happened. By the time he turned around I was almost at the top.

"Come back, babe," he snarled.

I slammed through the swinging fire door. Wiggsy swore and came after me, his feet crashing on the stairs, his heavy body creaking as he swayed from side to side.

I burst out onto the roof. It was dark, dark enough so that you couldn't see the aerials and chimneys and so forth except near the tops where they got high enough to be silhouetted against the light rising up from the city below. Wiggsy could hear me run, but he couldn't see me if I kept low.

The roofs were divided each from the other by low brick walls about two feet high. I couldn't tell how far the roofs went on. I began to run, ducking and dodging around the chimneys and the television aerials. I could tell where the aerials were by watching for the tops, which caught a bit of light, but the guy wires supporting them were invisible. They clawed at me, and sometimes they tripped me up and dumped me down on the rough tar, scraping my hands and bruising my kneecaps.

Behind me Wiggsy's heavy feet thumped like bass drums on the roof. He swore. "I'll get you, babe," he roared.

I crossed one roof and then another and then a third. When I figured I had a little lead I dashed for a fire door. It was locked. I ran on. Wiggsy pounded after me, cursing. I slipped over the wall onto the next roof and tried another fire door. It was locked, too. I ran on. Behind me I heard Wiggsy trip over something. He swore and got up. My legs were aching, and my chest burning. I kept on running, looking for a way out.

The trouble was that even when people didn't padlock the fire doors, they sometimes hooked them from the inside to keep them from blowing in the wind. It was easy enough to unhook them with a knife blade or a piece of wire; I had done it plenty of times before, fooling around on roofs with Stanky. But I had no wire and I had no knife and, besides, I didn't have any time. I crossed another roof and ran on.

Suddenly the roof ended. I came up to the last low wall and looked over. Five stories down below there was a parking lot, empty and dark. I whirled around. I couldn't see Wiggsy, but I could hear him stumbling along over the roofs, cursing and hollering and shouting my name. I whirled around again and, ducking low, ran along the wall toward the front of the building, looking for the fire escape. At the corner I hesitated. There was no wall along the front edge of the roof. I dropped flat, and peered over.

The streetlights were on below, putting a low shine on the tops of the cars rowed up along the curb. Small people coming home from work were going up and down the sidewalk, and two kids tore up the street, chasing each other.

The iron slatted platform at the top of the fire escape was a few feet farther along the edge of the roof. I did not dare stand up, for I would be silhouetted in the dim light coming up from below. I crawled toward it along the edge of the roof on my belly.

Wiggsy pounded across the roofs toward me. He had stopped shouting and cursing now, and he was panting so hard I could hear the rasp of breath in his throat across two roofs. He grunted, crossing the wall onto the last roof.

"Oh ho," he said triumphantly. "You run out of roofs, babe." He stopped dead, listening.

I lay frozen at the edge of the roof just above the iron slats of the fire escape platform three feet below. Wiggsy stood unmoving about fifty feet away. Lying flat, I could see the shape of his huge body against the city sky, his arms hanging loosely down by his round belly.

He looked around, turning his head this way and that, trying to spot me in the dark. Finally he began to move directly across the roof toward the last wall. As he walked he swiveled his head constantly from side to side, and every two or three paces he suddenly stopped, to listen for me.

I didn't dare move, but lay still, trying to breathe as quietly as possible, watching him come on.

He reached the far wall and moved along it a few paces. He was now pretty much behind me as I lay flat on the roof. I wriggled my head around a little to see where he was. My shoulder scraped on the rough tar.

He looked up and saw me faintly outlined on the edge of the roof. He dove for me, and I rolled off the roof and dropped down onto the iron platform at the top of the fire escape. His body slammed down onto the roof above me. I scrambled for the ladder going down. His big arm shot down toward me. I twisted toward the ladder.

He caught me by my collar and in one sweeping movement he jerked me sideways off the fire escape, and held me there, dangling at the end of his arm five stories above the side-walks.

"You know, babe," he said in that soft voice, "if I just opened my hand you'd go all the way down by yourself."

I raised my hands to grab on to his wrist, but he slapped them away with his free hand. He chuckled. "You'd just slide on down through the air with the greatest of ease, eh, babe? Slip right down there. Nothing to stop you but the cement at the bottom."

Suddenly he jerked me onto the roof and flung me down. "But if I threw you away like a bag of garbage a crowd would collect, and I don't think I want the publicity right now. No, I think I could do without the publicity." He paused. "Get up."

I stood up. Then he hit me. I didn't see it coming. The next thing I knew I was flat on the roof. My head rung and the side of my face was numb. "You pull another stunt like that and I'll give you one that'll take your head off. Get up. We're getting out of here."

He worked one of the fire doors open and we went down through the building to the street. I was dead tired. I'd been up since early in the morning, I'd done a terrific amount of walking, and I'd had hardly anything to eat all day. On top of it all, I'd been scared to death for hours. You stay scared like that for a long time, and it takes all the strength out of you.

Wiggsy wasn't taking any chances with me. Instead of going by cab, we walked across town to the Village. I didn't think I was going to make it. A couple of times my legs just gave way and I stumbled and fell down. When that happened Wiggsy picked me up and set me going again. He did it gently so that anyone going along the street wouldn't notice anything, but each time he'd give my arm another one of those warning squeezes.

He took me along Bleecker and up Sullivan Street and then down a narrow dark alleyway full of ash cans to hit at his shop from the rear. We landed in a tiny airshaft—about eight feet by four feet—that went up like a dark tower five stories high. Up at the top I could see a patch of light sky.

It was a dark, hidden place, a good place for strangling somebody, but he didn't do it. Instead he worked his way along the dark walls, dragging me by the hand to an iron door in the wall, which he pulled open. The door covered a low window hole which I guessed had been used to dump coal through in the old days.

Wiggsy crouched and listened by the window. Then he stepped back and motioned for me to climb through. I peered in. In the dim light from a distant bulb I could see a chair set below the window, and then a huge furnace surrounded by ash cans, like kids clustered around a grown-up. Wiggsy stuck his fist into my back. I dropped onto the chair and down to the floor in front of the furnace. Wiggsy slid in beside me and closed the iron door behind us.

The furnace was a monster which crouched under the low basement ceiling, with huge pipes leading away from its head like tentacles. Its skin was gray, and from around the edges of its mouth came the orange light of fire.

Wiggsy opened its door. The chamber inside was wide and deep and full of whirling, roaring flames. Wiggsy put his hand around the back of my neck and we stared at it, side by side. For a long time he didn't move, he didn't say anything, but stood there staring, and sucking on his cigarette which dangled from the corner of his mouth. The heat from the flames was hot on my face, and in a moment it was soaked with sweat. I watched the flames lash around in confusion, making a windy sound.

Finally Wiggsy flipped his cigarette butt into the boiling fire. The instant it touched the flames it disappeared. Then he put his hands around my neck and began to squeeze.

I shut my eyes and screamed; and when I opened them there was a policeman in a blue uniform standing in front of me with his pistol pointed straight into Wiggsy's face. For a fraction of a second I thought I was seeing things. Then Wiggsy flung me aside, and with one swift motion jerked the teddy bear out from under his shirt and flung it into the fire. It disappeared in the swirling flame and in a moment it was gone forever.

"Sapphires don't burn, Wiggsy," the cop said. "We'll get them later. Okay, let's go upstairs."

I didn't start crying until we got upstairs into Wiggsy's shop and I saw Pop. The place was crawling with cops and detectives. They were coming down the stairs, and in from the hal1, and up the front steps. They were all over the place. But I hardly saw them. Pop picked me up and hugged me. He looked like he was about to cry, too, but he didn't. I did the crying for both. Most times I would have been ashamed, but this time I wasn't: I figured I had it coming.

So then after a bit an ambulance came, and I

went outside and a young doctor in a white Ben Casey suit looked me over.

"There's nothing wrong with him," the doctor said, "but he looks pretty tired, and I'd just as soon put him in the hospital overnight."

I shook my head. "I can't go to the hospital. I've got to be on television in half an hour."

Pop laughed. "I think they'll forgive you this one time," he said.

But I wanted to go. "Please, Pop, they're counting on me. Please."

It was a dirty trick, for I knew that right then he'd do anything I wanted him to do, even burn a Jackson Pollock if I asked.

He looked at the doctor. The doctor shrugged.

"Please, Pop," I said. "The whole thing is only five minutes. Then I promise I'll go right to bed."

"It won't hurt him," the doctor said. "We'll take him up in the ambulance and wait for him."

So we got into the ambulance and went

peeling uptown through the traffic with the siren going full speed. I lay on a stretcher and rested and Pop told me what had happened.

Naturally, when he couldn't find me any-place, he called up Stanky to see if I was there. And then, after an hour or so, when I still didn't show up, Stanky had gotten scared and spilled the whole story: about the teddy, and the television show, and Wiggsy, and the gui-tar lessons, and the jewels—the whole thing. The story turned on the whole New York police force. They'd had a citywide alarm out for me, and of course they'd staked out Wiggsy's build-ing from top to bottom—including the furnace room. The cop who saved me had been hidden down behind the furnace just watching us to see what Wiggsy was going to do.

I'll be honest, I don't remember much about doing the television show. It all happened so fast. When I walked into the theater with Ben Casey and a couple of cops for an escort all the kids burst into cheers. Mr. Woodward and

Damon Damon, the Button King, bustled me into my costume and told me about all the last-minute changes they'd made. Then all at once we were out on the stage under the glare of bright lights going through our songs and doing the bad jokes with Jerry Wastebasket, and the audience was laughing and applauding. When suddenly it was over and we were off-stage and Damon Damon was whispering, "You were just mahvelous, dearies," and some other things that made Pop wince; and about five minutes after that I was in Manhattan General Hospital, falling asleep.

The big fuss came the next day. Of course they'd shut off Wiggsy's furnace and sifted the jewels out of the ashes. There was nothing for Wiggsy to do but confess, and naturally he squealed on his partners. According to his story he hadn't been in on the robbery at all. He had only been holding the jewels until they could be smuggled out of the country. You can believe that or not, however you like.

When Pop came to get me out of the hospital and take me home there were a mess of
reporters from the news papers and a couple of
cameramen from the television news programs. I
told them everything that happened, although
I admit I skipped over the teddy bear part of it
as much as I could: I just sort of slid over it. It
didn't help much, though. The next day the
newspapers started calling me "teddy bear
hero," and things like that. Man, the way they
wrote it up I was a big hero who'd saved the
Hermes Sapphire, instead of a kid who got himself into trouble by being dumb, and out of it by
being lucky.

That night Pop took me out to the Howard
Johnson's and filled me up with hamburgers and
all that jazz, and he let me go over to Crespino's
so I could see myself on the television there. He
even let me stay up late so I could see myself in
the news shows three times. The way my voice
sounded surprised me.

On Monday the kids kept clustering around

all day and staring at me and asking questions, and of course I was embarrassed and blushed most of the day; but not so embarrassed that I didn't manage to put on a casual pose and tell them that it wasn't anything, they'd have done the same themselves.

But then after school Stanky and I went over to his house and swiped some stuff out of his icebox and messed up his room with it, and after a while I began to feel normal again.

So that was the end of it. But of course nothing is ever over. This whole thing had two effects. One was that Pop bought me a Gretsch guitar and got me a good guitar teacher, after I promised to go on exposing myself to the finer music with Mr. Smythe-Jones.

The other effect was that I finally got the teddy bear off my back. Not that it didn't still make me nervous and embarrassed when I had to go in front of an audience. I got that feeling sometimes; but I didn't panic and go all to pieces anymore. You see, the teddy was dead and gone. I knew I had to get along without it, and I knew I could, for I'd done my whole part in the television show perfectly without it.

I guess I would have had to get used to it anyway. Mr. Woodward has got those of us who were on the show working up a little group of our own. He isn't making any prom-ises, but he thinks something might come of it. We rehearse Wednesdays after school, and then we all go down to the drugstore and drink Cokes and swagger around like a lot of big deals. We're beginning to sound pretty good. What we need now is a cool name. Mr. Woodward wanted to call us the Teddy Bears, but I talked him out of it. I've had enough of teddy bears to last me for a while.